I0818072

From *Prophecy Mates*

"Let's you and me get to know each other, Lady Mystery."

She gritted her teeth and told herself she was overreacting. *Flirt. Enjoy.* "Sure."

Zeus put an arm around her shoulders. His fingers traipsed along her collarbone until they took a walk on the wild side of her sternum, spelunking down her cleavage.

Enough was enough. She cleared her throat to make some classy excuse to beat his head into the wall.

Before she could, a buzz at the door distracted her. She glanced up as the crowd parted.

A blond man glided in like a panther, stopped, and stood there, as tall and confident as if he owned the place. He was built like a true Greek god, inverted triangle torso on long, strong legs. His golden hair shone lustrous in the electric light. His strong features accented by a rakish black mask drew the eye of every female in the room.

Zoe peeled off Zeus' arm and moved from him as if he'd never existed.

The blond man's gaze swung to her—and stopped.

The instant connection sang in her ears, in her blood, so powerful and shocking it kicked the air out of her lungs.

The man started toward her, cutting through the crowd like a sleek ship.

Her breath returned in quick, excited puffs.

His scent hit her as he neared, catapulting her back in time to cheerleading sweaters and smoking blunts in the woods...and the burnt scent of an almost-failed chemistry class.

"Damn my paws," she muttered.

Daniel Light.

“Wonderful characters take you on a marvelous journey through high school, treachery, conspiracy and a reconnected love. This story is fun, hot and just plain entertaining. Great read.” ~Amazon reviewer on *Prophecy Mates*

BOOK OF THE MONTH "I recommend reading this with a fan and ice water, because this one is hot enough to melt the screen of any device." ~ Foxglove, Long and Short Reviews on *Assassins Bite*

The masks are coming off.

Daniel Light is a powerful wizard prince on the hunt for a dangerous prophecy—only to find it’s in the hands of Zoe Blackwood, the woman he’d adored, and who’d firmly friend-zoned him, when he was a gangly teen. Daniel can get his hands on the prophecy by seducing Zoe at a masked ball, settling accounts with her. Yet he finds he wants to woo her.

Wolf shifter Zoe throws a classy, grand masked ball as her last chance at romance before her wolf forces her to mate. She remembers Daniel as that rich, awkward boy she could always count on yet never really noticed. When he shocks her by showing up at her ball, he's still rich but not awkward at all, and she notices his deadly grace plenty. But can she still count on him?

Then an evil fire wizard crashes the party, eager to get his hot hands on Zoe—and her prize, an ancient parchment. She’s horrified to discover both men are really after the parchment for its hidden prophecy—and she’s caught in the crosshairs.

Over the top, fun and action-packed, short and hot! If you like your heroes staunch, powerful, and faithful, this is the one for you!

Look for these titles by Mary Hughes

Now Available:

Romantic Adventure

Edie and the CEO—Crimson Romance

Falling ~~on~~ for the Billionaire

Cin Wikkid: April Fools For Love

Hot Chips and Sand

Bad Boy Billionaire's Lady: Lovless Brothers

Playing With Fire: The Battle of the Bands

Biting Love/The Ancients

Bite My Fire—Entangled

Biting Nixie—Entangled

The Bite of Silence—Entangled

Biting Me Softly—Entangled

Biting Oz—Entangled

Beauty Bites—Entangled

Downbeat—Entangled

Assassins Bite—Entangled

Passion Bites—Entangled

Biting Love Nibbles
Night's Caress—Entangled

Pull of the Moon Series
Prophecy Mates
Heart Mates
Hunt Mates
Mind Mates

Standalone
Black Diamond Jinn

Coming Soon:

The Classic Billionaire's Newshound (Lovless Brothers)
The Genius Billionaire's Hacker (Lovless Brothers)
Night's Kiss (The Ancients)
Night's Bliss (The Ancients)
Soul Mates (Pull of the Moon)

Prophecy Mates

Pull of the Moon

Mary Hughes

Prophecy Mates

ISBN: 978-1-940958-01-9
Print ISBN: 978-1-940958-03-3
Masked Attraction Cover by EJR Digital Art
Cover by Scott Carpenter

First electronic publication: February 2015
First print publication: February 2015
Second electronic publication: May 2017
First print publication: July 2017

DEDICATION

To Gregg, as they all are.

Thank you to Renee Wildes for her expertise and guidance on horses, and to Stacy D. Holmes for her expertise in manuscript assessment and gentle guidance editing. All mistakes are my own.

A heartfelt thank you to Nancy Gilliland for her expert beta reading and ending assist.

Chapter One

Looking back, wizard prince Daniel Light would wonder if the run of bad luck that Halloween had been a portent.

Or if Fate just had a particularly malicious sense of humor.

"Terrible unknown prophecy ticking, two hours to find it—so of course there's not a single open parking space in sight." Daniel glared at the packed line of cars as he sped his Ferrari alongside Lake Michigan's lapping waters. "Although, what do I expect on Halloween, good luck?"

As if taunting him, a flash of open curb appeared—on the opposite side of the road. Swearing, Daniel barged into the left lane then cranked a U-turn the instant there was a break in traffic. Nearly a quarter mile had passed.

Urgently scanning for the space, hoping nobody nabbed it first, he sped south on Lincoln Memorial Drive. He had to find that prophecy tonight. It could only be claimed on Halloween.

Two hours to midnight.

The space opened up suddenly between a student's small sedan and an oversized jacked-up SUV. Breathing a sigh of relief, he darted into the gap.

And stomped on the brakes. The Ferrari nearly stood on its nose.

The SUV was parked over the line, eating up half the space. Its vanity plate read RD HOG. Daniel could only fit the front half of his car in, his back half sticking out in traffic.

Behind him, a disgruntled horn blew.

"Lovely. As if tonight wasn't already shaping up to be the bastard merger of a wind farm and a manure factory." Shrugging off his frustration, he shifted into reverse. He'd have to try farther down the road.

He got two inches. The car behind him had crept up until it was on his bumper. Three cars stacked up behind, adding their angry beeps. A solid line of traffic in the through-lane kept them all penned in like an electric fence.

"Hells bells." His hands tightened on the steering wheel. Talk about the rock, the hard place, and stuck.

The only solution that occurred to him was the one he couldn't use. Magic would've solved this problem in a jiffy, if he'd had enough time to prepared a spell.

But improvise? Magic was too complex. Touchy. Drained a lot of personal energy. Witches almost always cast tried-and-true spells or triggered imbued objects. It was safer.

An irate car-horn chorus built up behind him. Daniel's shoulder tension built with it. Trying to ignore both the noise and the clock, he wracked his brain for a solution.

Nothing came to mind.

"Not a good idea," he muttered even as he took out his wand. But magic was the only idea he had, good or not, and time was ticking. A simple spell, a tiny push to smoothly shift the SUV back, should work. As a wizard prince, he ought to have enough energy and talent to pull it off without incident.

Hopefully.

He pointed the wand at the SUV. "By air and earth, by moonlight's shine," he intoned, drawing power from deep inside himself and feeding it into the words. "Move that bastard back in line."

A twitch of the wand released the spell.

Sure enough, the oversized vehicle slid back. Daniel grinned. "Ha. Halloween isn't such sucky luck..."

Crunch. RD HOG smacked into the car behind it.

Daniel winced. "Or maybe not."

As he shoehorned his car into the gap, the backed-up traffic released and shooped angrily past him—with a few fingers of greeting. He shook his head with a rueful smile, not blaming them in the least. He felt rather the same way. Sliding from the car, he loped back to examine the damage. At least he'd found a space.

Although, from the crumpled back of the SUV, he'd be paying a hefty price for it.

He tucked his business card under the SUV's windshield wiper. It was a small enough cost if he could recover the prophecy.

Possibly the greatest—or worst—of Avignon's *lost* prophecies.

"The Avignon Quatrain," the family seer had said. *"It's at Villa Terrace."*

Turning to the bluff, he looked up...and up. Stairs climbed into the night sky itself. The imposing villa mansion was its crown.

Even athletes would find that climb challenging; Daniel had been a gangly, nerdy teen. Though he was fit enough now, having made himself over to win the love of a girl.

Damn, he hadn't thought about Zoe in *years*...well, months...okay, not for days at least.

Pushing her from his mind, he called on the muscles he'd painstakingly built and filled his lungs with air. Time to see how far he'd really come in life.

He dashed up the first set of stairs, taking them two at a time, muscles working fluidly, breath coming easily. His heart was only beating marginally harder as he paused in a lower garden to pull a Zorro-style black mask from his tuxedo's jetted side pocket.

Tonight's disguise. He tied it on.

The family seer's urgent phone call a few hours ago told him where and when. Villa Terrace, tonight only, no encores. But there was a problem—there was an event going on there, a posh masked ball given by an enigmatic Queen of Hearts. He'd had just enough time to don his tux and drive to Milwaukee.

Suitably camouflaged, Daniel bounded lightly up one of a pair of angle-bracket stairs.

Emerging on top of the upper terrace, he threaded through sumptuous sculpture and topiary to join a swarm of women in silky gowns and men in severe suits. The river of rich carried him into the villa.

The ballroom doors inside were provocatively closed. The glitterati milled, breathless with excitement, for the event to start. Romance was in the air.

Daniel ignored it. He simply needed to blend in, to give himself time and space to hunt down the prophecy.

He didn't want to romance anyone.

Memory of Zoe's rich mahogany hair, gorgeous curves, and generous smile assaulted him.

"Smack me sideways," he muttered under his breath. "Job to do. Not thinking about her."

* * *

"The champagne fountain! Dammit, Dorine, I forgot to turn it on." Zoe Singer Blackwood, public owner of Zoe's Harleys and More and secretly a wolf shifter, sailed through the back of the ballroom, dodging wait staff tending laden buffet tables.

"I'm sorry, Ms. Blackwood." The stalwart event planner, clutching her ever-present clipboard, scurried to keep pace. "That was my job."

"Your job—my responsibility. I'm not expecting much from tonight's crop of bachelors, so I'd like everything else to be as romantic as possible. Speaking of..." Zoe caught sight of her nearly naked breasts in the gold-encrusted wall mirrors. She tugged up the spangled bodice of her little black strapless number. On the model, it was cut to showcase feminine assets; on Zoe's lush figure, it was a rubber band with a ruffle. "I love your taste in decorations. Your advice on clothes, not so much. I want to make romance, not a porno."

"Still getting dressed?" Her cousin Noah spoke in her Bluetooth earbud, his deep voice amused. "Hasn't your shindig already started?"

"Bite me, Noah." She adjusted the earpiece, trying not to tangle it in her mask's elastic. The phone itself was in her purse in one of the nearby prep rooms. For the first time, she wished the earbud's range wasn't quite so far. "Just because you're going to be my alpha one day doesn't mean I can't kick you where it counts."

He laughed. "That's the Zoe I know and love. So why are you doing this ball, again? Seems a little, I don't know, out of character."

Why, indeed? She headed for the center table dominated by a three-tiered crystal fountain, currently dark and silent. Crawling under a white-linen tablecloth, she flipped the fountain's rocker switch.

The burble of liquid started, then splashed as champagne cascaded. She backed out. "It's hard to explain."

Dorine was staring at her backside, embarrassment clear on her maskless face.

"You might be right about the dress," the planner said. "Um, cute panties."

Zoe gave her a rueful smile as she stood, brushing hands and knees, then tugged down her hem. Upstairs, her breasts bobbled dangerously. She sighed, giving up. "How's the rest of that checklist?"

"Decorations complete, food laid out." Dorine's red face ebbed as she ticked efficiently on her clipboard. "Bars fully stocked, staff here, orchestra assembling. We're ready."

"Thanks, Dorine. For everything. The place looks enchanting."

With a small, pleased smile, the planner left.

"Why a ball?" Noah asked in her ear.

Because she'd had one glimpse of romance, in high school. One rich, classy, untouchable boy amid all the under-the-bleacher gropes. Daniel Light. He'd shown her what real devotion was, the kind that didn't have sex strings attached. That sweet-down-to-her-toes feeling was unforgettable. She was trying to recreate it with a rich, classy ball.

But she didn't know how to say all that in a way Noah would understand. She tried, "A ball is romantic. Sophisticated."

"You want romance? Wasn't MatchShift.com good enough?"

"Noah, I'm twenty-nine. You know what that means. When I hit thirty, my wolf will *force* me to take a mate."

"You've given up finding Mr. Right?"

"Or even Mr. Good Enough. In one year, I'll get Mr. Pup Daddy whether I want him or not." She shuddered at the thought. Mated wolves pawed at each other constantly. "First I want Some Enchanted Evenings." Before it was too late, she'd kindle romance then hang onto that feeling with everything she was.

"You're a shifter, Zoe. You have your pick of men."

"My wolf gets me plenty of sex—and don't get me wrong, I *like* sex—but I've seen too many beds and couches and tabletops. My human knows there's more. Roses and poetry and walks on moonlit beaches."

"On Lake Michigan? More like pebbles in your paws."

How to explain why this was so important? "Noah, this party isn't just about me. This is for all the women like me who've had enough of groping guys. Women who want a few candles and cuddles first." She started a last sweep of the room, resplendent in its red silk streamers, sweet-smelling flowers, champagne, and choice tidbits of shrimp, cheese, and *petits fours*. "I've got an orchestra with real strings and everything. If guys can't get their romance on with all this, they're not trying."

Noah snorted his disbelief. "Throwing a ball with nice clothes and live music isn't going to stop men from being men."

"Maybe, but I have a cunning plan."

"Saltpeter in the mashed potatoes?" he suggested. "Meat-cleaver vasectomy?"

"Ha. No, I'm offering a prize to whoever romances me the best. Or rather, the Queen of Hearts is offering it. And here's the best part. Since we're *all* masked, the guys won't know who the Queen of Hearts is. The men *can't* be men. They'll have to court all the women here. Cool, or what?"

"Cool," Noah admitted. "But what's the prize?"

"The Singer Parchment."

He sucked in a breath. "Your family heirloom?"

"Sixteenth century French calligraphic art at its best." She turned toward the crown of the evening, safe in its locked glass case at the foot of the bubbling champagne fountain. "From the late House of Valois period. My father had it authenticated."

She started toward the case, intending to admire the parchment's black swirling letters and full-color, illuminated capitals.

The key stood in the lock. Anyone could turn it and snatch the prize.

She straightened abruptly and shouted, "Dorine. Key!"

"Ow." Noah's voice was pained.

"Sorry. Damn my paws, where is that planner? Everything will be ruined if there's no prize." She flew to the case, plucked out the small key, and dropped it in her décolletage.

"But why an antique? Wouldn't men respond better to stadium tickets or free beer?"

"Seriously? My kind of 'man' would respond better to chasing rabbits in the woods. I want a different type of guy, one interested in the finer things in life."

"Considering the males you normally date, you know this, how?"

"I met a nice boy, once," she tried to explain. "A rich boy. His parents threw a lavish, romantic Halloween ball. White tie, orchestra, parchment party favors, the works—and a genuine antique door prize. Absolutely magical. I'm trying to recreate that magic." She'd invited two hundred of the city's most sophisticated, eligible singles. Then she personally invited the women from the local shelter where she volunteered. She wanted to give them the same chance she'd had—a glimpse of something better.

To know, at least once, what it was like to be wooed by a truly attentive man.

"That parchment has been in your family for generations. I'm surprised your mother agreed to it."

"It's mine," Zoe said quickly. "Dad's family. Mom was just holding it for me."

A surprised pause. Then he growled, "Zoe."

She winced. "Yeah, okay. Mom doesn't actually know. Please don't blab to her. I had to, Noah. You know that round little woman who runs the weird bookstore in Matinsfield, with all the crystals and stuff?" Zoe's home pack was based in Matinsfield in northern Wisconsin.

"Linda Blue? Only by reputation."

"She's a fortuneteller on the side. I bumped into her on my last visit home, and she told me I needed to get rid of the parchment *or else*."

"Or else what?"

She opened her mouth to tell him. Linda Blue said if Zoe didn't get rid of the parchment—on Halloween, no less—an evil witch would come and kill whoever possessed it. Shifters couldn't identify witches on sight, so she took the parchment to protect her mom.

But if Zoe told Noah that, he'd be on the first transport here, trying to protect *her*.

"Oh, you know seers. Gotta pump up the doom. It's probably nothing." She peered into the display case, expecting to see the usual four words, COEUR, ESPRIT, ÂME, CLÉ. Heart, mind, soul, and key.

Letters blazed across the top, *Give this to the Light, Zoe*—then poofed the instant she'd read them.

Her heart leaped into her throat, pushing her breath out on a gasp.

Noah caught it. "Zoe? *What's* going on?" His growl wasn't the cousin requesting information, it was the alpha-to-be demanding it.

Her wolf whined in response, and even her human winced. How could she dodge this silver bullet?

"Sorry, time to open the doors. Loveyoubuhbye!" She clicked off and tucked the small earpiece next to the key in her cleavage—plenty of room, with her measurements.

Then, because she didn't want to be a liar, she took a few steps toward the doors, waving at the greeters to open them.

Tuxedoed men and women in exotic dresses flowed into the room.

Zoe smoothed hands along hips, her stomach churning with both nerves and excitement. It surprised her; her wolf wasn't usually jumpy. A good run would take care of that, but she couldn't leave her guests.

A man in a ripped black leather cowl broke off from the mob, making a beeline toward her.

Her nerves twanged. This was it. She'd wanted romance, and here came her first chance. She pasted on a quick smile.

He blew past her, headed straight for the parchment case.

Her smile dropped and she palmed her nape. Twist her tail, this evening was *not* starting well. What else could go wrong?

As if in response, the crowd parted. Zoe looked up, stomach twisting at some new unexpected difficulty.

A tall blond man glided into the ballroom like a panther instead.

Her stomach abruptly stopped twisting. Fascination tugged at her as her heart burst into a fast staccato rhythm.

He was built like a Greek god, inverted triangle torso on long, strong legs. His golden hair shone lustrous in the electric light. Stark features, accented by a rakish black mask, drew the eye of every female in the room.

The blond man's gaze swung to Zoe—and stopped.

Connection sang in her blood, rang in her ears, so powerful it shocked the air out of her lungs.

The man started toward her, cutting through the crowd like a sleek ship.

Her breath returned in quick, eager puffs. This man exuded romance with a capital R. His masked eyes were a gorgeous blue, spokes of silver around each pupil like exploding stars. His hair was bright blond, like sunshine.

She couldn't wait to talk to him, touch him, *kiss* him... Although something about that hair and those eyes were familiar.

As he neared, his scent hit her. The smell catapulted her back in time, to cheerleader sweaters and smoking blunts in the woods...

And the burnt scent of an almost-failed chemistry class.

"Damn my paws," she muttered.

Daniel Light.

Chapter Two

Daniel knew how to make an entrance. He stepped into the ballroom with confidence, smiling and nodding.

But his mind was on the prophecy, wondering what form it took. Book, painting, scroll, or something else? Whatever it was, it'd be sixteenth century and French. That was the era of Jean-Dion d'Avignon, founding wizard prince of the Witches' Council and one of the most powerful witches ever.

Lost prophecy? Most likely hidden, then, whatever form it's taking. He'd have to find his way into the private areas of the villa, perhaps through the three doors in back of the ballroom.

Then the crowd parted.

She stood there.

The rest of the room faded until bright light haloed her and only her. Spring-green eyes shone against the black of her domino mask. Glossy hair rippled like a living mahogany waterfall. Her lush figure was banded provocatively in black glitter. She held herself with the sensuous grace of a lioness.

Daniel's his heart leaped and began to pound, his blood heating until it almost boiled. His groin stirred with hunger.

He'd never seen a more beautiful female in his life.

He launched toward her with a lion's hunting prowl. As he neared, her scent hit him, a complex mixture of jasmine, saffron, and woman.

That scent...

High school memories crowded him. His breath caught as he took one last stuttering step toward her. Her voluptuous body, her sweet smile, her kind soul had given him life...and the most erotic dreams a boy ever had. Or a man still had.

Zoe Blackwood.

It was a measure of how hard the sight of her hit him that he didn't question her being here. He simply drank in the sight of her. His mouth dropped open, but he couldn't seem to care. Zoe had been a gorgeous young woman; time had only sharpened her appeal, honing her features and adding the sparkle of wit and wisdom to her eyes, green like new grass and even more startling against her black domino.

And, oh yeah, her curves were now so lush his hands itched to shape them through that painted-on thing she wore.

He swallowed a sudden influx of saliva. Nearly choked on his swollen, hot tongue. His hands weren't the only things that wanted to slick along her curves. On the plus side, swallowing forced him to shut his idiotic mouth.

Her eyes widened in her mask, gaze riveted on him.

She's *interested* in me. His groin tightened painfully.

He'd dreamed of this moment a thousand times over the years. He'd made himself over exactly so that if he met her again, he'd have a second chance.

His brain smacked him upside the head. *Interested? Or is that horror that the high school dork is back?*

That cooled him faster than a bucket of ice.

It also brought his brain back online, enough that he wondered what she was doing here. Earth and wilderness seemed more her element than city society and a fancy ball.

Probably running things. That was what Zoe did best. And if she was running this shindig, that meant she was the Queen—

She smiled at him.

The sensuous curve of her coral lips kicked his intellect out of the driver's seat. Years of hope and dreams roared to life. Time to test dreams against reality. *Time to impress her, Light.* He glided toward her until only inches and a breathless silence separated them.

"Lovely lady." He towered over her as he'd never done in high school, and she gave a delicious shiver.

"Handsome gentleman." She offered her hand.

He lifted it to his lips, lingering over her soft skin and luscious scent. Just as he remembered, but with a deeper, darker feminine note. "My name is—"

"No names tonight."

Her voice was as lyrical as he remembered, too, with an added sexy breathiness.

"I'll be Lady Mystery. And you can be My Hero." She touched her left hand to his tux-covered biceps.

He straightened, his muscles pumping with vigor, his body swelling with pride. She'd always done that to him. Made him feel stronger than he was, better.

Did she know that? Did she even realize, when she was kind to him in high school, that she was the first to see past his gangly, sand-kicked-face exterior to the heart of the hero inside? Did she know that, over a thousand small touches and gestures in chemistry class, he'd fallen in love with her, and *she* was the reason he'd made himself over into the image of a superstud?

One way to find out.

"No names," he agreed. "But clichés aside, haven't we met before?"

"Oh, no." Her smile ripened. "I wouldn't forget a man like you."

She doesn't know me. A small part of him was disappointed.

Then, as she gazed up at him, her green eyes went nearly black, and her glossy lips parted.

As if she wanted to kiss him.

A wash of desire boiled through his veins. She didn't know him? Yeah, that only meant he had a blank slate with her. A clean page to write a new story, one where he impressed the hell out of her.

A new tale, where he showed himself as a man worthy of Zoe Blackwood's love.

As if she was on the same page, her fingers slid enticingly along his arm, her eyes heating. "I don't know about you, but..." Her voice was lusciously throaty. "This feels magical."

Desire flamed through him. Worthy of her love, worthy of *making love* to her. He hungered to take her, bend her over the crisp linen covered table, and give her a climax so hard she'd shatter...

Magical?

The prophecy. Blasted bats and broomsticks.

Daniel groaned silently. He'd made himself a jock and filthy rich to impress this very woman.

Yet he couldn't romance Zoe now, he couldn't even take her out for a cup of tea. He had less than two hours to find the prophecy.

His heart contracted painfully. He wanted to be Zoe's romantic hero, so much it burned. But the prophecy...well.

Avigon's divinations tended to end less in kitten-has-a-sad and more in apocalyptic, shambling, end-of-the-world horrors. The Avignon Quatrain, especially if the wrong witch got his hands on it?

The end of the world as they knew it.

Much as Daniel wanted to be Zoe's romantic hero, he'd have to be a real hero. He had to tear himself away from her and find that prophecy.

Acid disappointment ate at him as he released her fingers. It was unutterably hard.

A puzzled frown replaced her enchanted expression, and her hand dropped to her side.

Now walk away.

His feet wouldn't move.

Damn it, he was a wizard prince, with all that implied. He had willpower and concentration enough to restrain a demon. Surely, he could step away from the lush temptation that was Zoe Blackwood?

Yeah, he did. Made him feel like crap, but he murmured an excuse, wheeled, and made himself walk away.

* * *

Zoe blinked in stunned surprise at Daniel's broad back, disappearing into the throng. What had just happened?

The boy whose feelings you ignored in high school gave you a taste of your own medicine.

She groaned. It didn't matter that she hadn't *meant* to be insensitive, that, at the time, she was just a young girl with painfully adult issues.

Her heart squeezed hard. She'd managed to push away the hurt from that time and get on with her life. Seeing him again brought it all back.

Wiping hot eyes, she turned away. She'd been so shocked to see him, then so insanely attracted to him, that she hadn't wondered why he was here. Perhaps one of her invited guests had brought him. It was his kind of shindig.

Momentarily she felt better. *I got the ambiance right.*

Then the truth hit her. She'd thought she done this ball to imitate of Daniel's parents, to attract men like Daniel. But seeing him again...

She'd done this ball to *attract Daniel.*

Shocked, chagrined, at first she didn't see the man in the ripped, stitched-leather mask, bent over the parchment case.

Ripped-Mask caressed the case as if studying it intently—or maybe trying to make out with it.

Agitation launched her toward him. Even if she'd done this ball for Daniel, he'd walked away from her.

He doesn't want me anymore... Maybe I'm not good enough for him. Maybe I never was. A surprising amount of pain hit her. She swallowed it and marched determinedly toward Ripped-Mask. Daniel had left, but there were plenty of classy men in the forest.

If Ripped-Mask was interested in the parchment, that meant he was classy, right?

Donning her best Mona Lisa smile, she pitched her voice low and sultry, trying for sexy. "Hello."

The word came out just short of *Lookin' for a good time, sailor?* She winced and had enough time to think, *This isn't such a good idea* when he jerked toward her as if annoyed.

The cowl masked his head and cheeks but exposed a brutal mouth and jaw. Piggy eyes showed through small, mismatched holes.

His gaze dropped precipitously, catching on her breasts and heating as lustfully as if he had X-ray vision.

She had to work to keep her smile in place. "I'm Lady Mystery."

"Not much mystery," he growled, chainsaw-rough—then he pointed at her bared cleavage.

As if she was in danger of missing his clever wit.

Then his gaze rose and he smiled, and he was almost handsome. He held out his hand. "Zeus."

The name of the top-of-the-food-chain Greek god. No lack of ego there.

Still, that flirting wasn't going to do itself. She took his hand, meaning to shake it briefly, but he tightened his grip and tugged her closer.

"Let's you and me get to know each other, Lady Mystery." He rubbed a palm over her bare arm.

Her belly fluttered. Not all of it was attraction. To her wolf's heightened senses, he reeked of testosterone, the kind filled with anger and ambition.

She gritted her teeth and told herself she was overreacting. *Flirt. Enjoy.* "Sure."

He dropped an arm over her shoulders and pulled her into his side. He was solidly built and Zoe told herself she liked the feel of him.

Then his fingers traipsed down her collarbone.

She tried to make a classy joke of it. "Hey, now. That's a little too fast. There's getting to know you, and then there's getting to know *all* about you—"

"Like this?" His fingers spelunked into her cleavage.

"That's *enough.*" She grabbed his wrist, about to make some classy excuse to beat his head into the wall.

A cry distracted her.

"Get off me!"

Female, high, stressed. To her right.

Zoe's wolf zoomed in on a slight figure in a simple, silver lamé sheathe at a nearby hors d'oeuvre table. A woman from the shelter.

A Romeo in a marquess's sash with enough medals to be its own platoon backed the woman into the table. He slurred, "I'm being romantic. Women like the strong, forceful type."

"Not like this." The woman slapped at the marquessy guy, her flailing arms sending the table's rose petals and heart-shaped confetti flying. "Stop it!"

Zoe tossed off Zeus' arm and headed for her.

"Just one kiss." The sashed guy grabbed the woman's lamé and puckered up.

"She said *stop*." Zoe seized the guy's arm and yanked it like the string of a yo-yo.

He spun away from the woman, straight into Zoe's glare. To make sure he got the message, she put a little wolf into it.

His mask-on-a-stick dropped to swing from its ribbon, his mouth a surprised O. The alcohol fumes surrounding him stung Zoe's nose like a liquor smog. The guy was practically one hundred proof. Either he'd loaded up before coming, or in the few seconds since the doors had opened, he'd gone diving in the champagne fountain.

"Need help?" Daniel's deep voice came from nearby.

Daniel. I can still count on him. A little flutter of relief trilled through her. "Thanks, but I can handle this." To the marquessy guy she said, "You're done." She marched him toward the door, trying not to breathe too deeply.

"Wh-why?" He stared blurrily up at her. "I was romancing her."

"Romance does *not* mean feeling up a woman like a Japanese body pillow." She marched him toward the greeters, picking the biggest man tending the door. "Escort this gentleman out, would you?" She'd have applied boot to butt if her dress hadn't been in danger of doing a window-shade roll up. After all, Daniel was somewhere behind her. She didn't want to look like an undignified idiot.

* * *

Daniel had been searching the farthest corners of the ballroom, even discreetly getting down on his knees to throw a glance under the orchestra's stage, when he'd heard the woman's cry. He'd gotten here in time to see Zoe handle it in her usual forthright manner.

She was remarkably capable; she always had been. Warmth surged through him, pride and something more.

As she marched Count Von Blotto out, it occurred to Daniel that Zoe's competence might be his best chance at uncovering the prophecy. She'd had a knack for finding every popular and secret haunt in high school. If anyone would know the nooks and crannies of this place, it was her.

All he had to do was ask for her help.

His solution had nothing to do with the fact that then he could spend more time with her.

Probably.

* * *

Zoe turned to find Daniel there, approval warming his eyes. "You don't need anybody's help, do you?"

She nearly blurted, *I was grateful for yours in high school.* She managed to stop herself in time. "I try not to."

"I could use yours, though. How well do you know this place?"

Heat crept into her face. He didn't recognize her as Zoe, but could he know she was the Queen of Hearts? "Why would you think I know it?"

"You ordered the greeter to get rid of that troublemaker. I'm guessing you're in charge."

"I'm one of the party planners," she equivocated.

"I've heard so much about the hidden places of Villa Terrace, but I've never actually seen them. I'd love to have the private tour, if you know what I mean."

"Oh. *Oh.*" The word *private* conjured up all sorts of hungry ideas. Her cheeks heated—along with other parts of her.

And she *liked* it. Yes, tonight was supposed to be about romance, not sex. But Daniel had never asked for her help before. Only given his, without expectation of return. He'd helped her when she'd needed him most. She'd passed chemistry because of him. Any other boy she knew would've expected something in return.

Daniel was the one boy who hadn't helped just to get in her pants.

She'd underestimated that selfless aid then. Didn't really appreciate the cute-but-scrawny kid with the clunky glasses who saw she was struggling and stepped in—not for any reward, but simply to make her life better.

She'd thanked him, but she'd never acknowledged what it cost him. With the self-centeredness of youth, she'd never thought to do anything in return, never asked if he needed help or invited him to a party or even gone and bought him coffee.

She ached at her stupidity, now. She'd come to realize, too late, that he'd probably had feelings for her. That her indifference might have hurt him. Not intentional, but it was one reason she'd never tried to reconnect with him, not wanting to reopen any wounds. That, and the guilt that pushed her to think she didn't deserve him.

But now?

She'd changed since high school. Now, she appreciated character as much as brawn.

No, more. She'd created this classy, romantic ball to attract him. Subconsciously, but he was here. Why not take advantage of that? Why not do everything in her power to prove to them both that she deserved someone as classy, intelligent, and handsome as him?

New excitement bubbled up inside her. "I'd love to help you."

He smiled down at her. *Down* at her. Her belly shimmied. She'd changed, but he'd changed too, grown tall and muscular.

A hunger surged inside her, to help him, to give him his private tour—and to do all the things *private* implied. To thrust her hands into his bright hair, bring his chiseled jaw down to her, and press her lips against his. To open her mouth to him, craving the rough caress of his tongue, driving past her lips. To press herself wantonly against his tall body and flatten her curves against the rock-solidness of those muscles.

And she knew exactly where to start. "Come with me."

Intrigue lit his eyes.

Three access doors serviced the back of the ballroom. She led him out the middle one, down a short hallway, and into the decorations prep room.

Empty now, decorators gone and tables pushed against the walls, the room was cool. A chill passed over Zoe's flesh, leaving doubt in its wake. As with Zeus, maybe she was making a mistake.

"What's behind here?" He stalked past her toward a folding screen in the corner. His scent wafted into her nose, tangy, masculine.

This is Daniel, not Zeus. The boy I could always count on. I'm not making a mistake.

She followed. "Just a fainting couch..." Where he could press her into the cushions with his now-heavy body. Where her passionate kiss could spin into a wildfire of lust. Where she could spread her aching thighs and feel his weight sink between... Her words trailed off as a burst of desire electrified her pelvis.

He turned just in time to catch it. Surprise lit his blue eyes.

For one instant she faltered. Maybe he really had only wanted her help searching out the nooks and crannies. Maybe she'd only imagined he was as greedy for her as she was for him.

Then his pupils dilated and his eyes darkened hungrily behind his mask. "Lady Mystery..." His voice was deliciously husky.

Her spirits and desire roared back to life. Her lips began to throb. She touched her tongue to her lower lip.

His gaze dropped to her mouth and fired hot as twin sapphire suns.

And suddenly she was kissing him with an insatiable hunger.

* * *

Daniel had dreamed for years of kissing Zoe Blackwood, waking with tangled sheets and dampened skin. Sweet dreams.

Reality was even sweeter, and much, much hotter. Her mouth scorched him like cinnamon. He wrapped his arms around her, her body small and soft yet strong. Her arms twined around his neck in return. Surprisingly, she had to lift herself to do it. She'd seemed so regally tall in high school. Now, he commanded her by half a foot or more. He loved the way she stretched herself against him, opening to him.

He cupped her head to press her closer, taking her mouth deeper. Her hair streamed through his fingers like silky warm water.

She released a soft moan. The hungry sound resonated deep inside him, desire igniting his very cells.

Zoe pressed into him, her breasts pillowed against him, full and ripe. Then she rubbed herself against him like a cat.

He shuddered with a powerful response. Almost beastlike himself, he crushed her bountiful, feminine body against him. A growl rose low in his throat, a rumbling of possession. A sudden urge filled him, to nip down her neck, brand her taste on his tongue, mark her with his scent...

* * *

Zoe's wolf howled joyously as she rubbed wantonly against Daniel's strength. He felt so good, so right, so *wolfish*.

He nipped down her jaw, the sharp sensation driving straight to her wolf's core.

She kicked back her head in response, craving his teeth on her throat, wanting the edge that signaled an alpha's possession.

His mouth moved down to the soft skin of her neck, hot breath billowing.

Yes. Do it. Take *me.*

He nipped her gently.

A howl of triumph rose in her throat. *Mine.* She opened her mouth to let her wolf's voice free.

Daniel isn't pack. He's human.

She hesitated, howl stuck awkwardly in her throat. She'd let her wolf out with a human only once before, when she was young.

She'd gotten fear and hatred in return.

Beast.

"Don't stop." His chest rumbled against her, an animal growl rolling through *him.* His tongue thrust into her mouth, meeting her own, just short of savage. Claiming her as roughly as a wolf.

As powerfully as an *alpha.*

It reignited her hunger. She speared him with her own tongue, the kiss battling hot and unrestrained, each trying to take more. *Give* more.

"You're so perfect," he rasped. "Smell, feel, taste."

"Too much talking." Zoe practically tore open his tux jacket to drive her hands underneath and grab his torso. She seized the hardest muscles in the world. Her wolf's claws tried to grow at the feel, and she barely restrained them. He just felt so good.

Daniel groaned and slanted his head to tongue her deeper, driving into the cavern of her mouth. Lust shocked her system, a bright jolt riding to the ends of her nerves. She took all he had to give and opened wider.

Asking for even more.

He seized her head in both hands and gave it to her, driving powerfully into her mouth, again and again. Flames licked her body. She was panting. His chest pumped against her too, dragging satin lapels and superfine wool and pearl-and-onyx buttons back and forth over her sensitized flesh.

Shivers chased along her skin. She rippled against him, licking and kissing his mouth, cheek, jaw, greedily tasting everything she could reach.

Asking for still more.

Backing her into the fainting couch, he pushed her down, and she reveled in his strength.

But she was strong, too. Her wolf helped flip him, and she climbed on top. From the bulge in his slacks, he was equally excited by her taking charge.

She leaned over and grinned into his masked face.

Something flickered in his eyes, scorching hot. Like a wolf of his own seized him—or his soul ignited.

He flipped her, too strong and fast to counter even if she'd wanted. But she enjoyed the breathless sensation, trapped under his weight. Her wolf could have shoved him off, but neither of them wanted to be anywhere but under him.

Then he thumbed down one cup of her bodice, exposing her breast tip furled tight in need. She moaned and arched. His eyes flared in his mask, his gaze greedy on her exposed flesh. He growled again, dark and possessive. Hot desire shot through her.

His head lowered.

Zoe panted in anticipation. His head blocked her view, but she felt the heat of his breath roll over her skin and she whimpered her encouragement.

"My Hero. I want you to..." She thrust herself toward him.

He flicked eyes shot with starfire up at her. Gaze locked on hers, his lips touched her skin. *Relief*... But instead of pulling her aching tip into his mouth, he pressed tiny kisses to her soft skin, gentle little butterflies.

Her frustration ripped from her throat in a growl. She didn't want gentle, not from him, not after her animal was unleashed. Threading fingers in his bright hair, she urged him to do more, harder.

He resisted, kissing and nibbling ever so lightly.

More. Her fingers tightened in his hair until she was nearly ripping strands.

And he... he only traced sweet little circles around the puckered tip.

Her body bowed up under him. "*Please.*" She tugged hard on his head, trying to pull him where she wanted him to go. She wanted to scream. *Lick me. Suckle me.* Bite *me.*

"Demanding, aren't we?" He chuckled—and finally sucked her into his hot mouth.

"*Yes,*" she hissed. "More. *More!*"

He nipped. His sharp teeth sent pangs of longing straight to her sex. In desperation, she grabbed both cups of her dress and yanked down, pulling open the back zipper.

The hands-free earpiece tumbled out and hit the floor. *Clack.*

But no metallic ding of key.

He cupped her naked breasts in his palms, his skin hot, his gaze reverent. "You're so beautiful. I imagined this for so long..."

"My key." Barely listening, she half-sat in the cage of his body, frantically combing the floor with her gaze. "Where's the key?"

"Key?" His lids rose, lust glazing his eyes. "What key?"

"To the prize case." She dug a hand into her hair, wincing as her claws grooved her scalp. "I tucked it in my bodice earlier. It must have fallen out when I...when we...or maybe before we..." She groaned. "It doesn't matter when. I need to find that key. Will you help me?"

Slowly, he shook his golden head. "I have my own hunt."

"You don't understand." She grabbed his head to stop his no. "If I lose the parchment, this whole evening's for nothing. Daniel, you have to help me, please."

He sucked air at the name. The glaze of lust in his eyes abruptly cleared and he released her breasts.

In her agitation, that was the first she realized she'd said *Daniel*, revealing she knew him. Reluctantly, she met his gaze.

The masked blue eyes, shrewd and intelligent, were shot with ice instead of fire.

"When did you figure out it was me?" His tone was neutral.

"Almost right away." Her face felt hot and prickly, as if she was perspiring. "I knew it was you because...well." How did she say she'd never forgotten his scent without sounding like a perv? She took the first human-sounding reason that hit her. "Your mask. It reminded me of those dorky glasses you used to wear."

The absolute wrong thing to say. She knew it the moment it left her mouth.

He leaped to his feet, his color high. “I knew it was you, too, but that’s why I didn’t tell you. I’m sorry. I didn’t mean to take advantage of you, but it was so nice, you treating me as if I were one of the popular boys you used to date.” He turned away.

He’s leaving me. Hurt stabbed her. “Daniel, don’t go. Please? I need help.” She stopped him the only way she knew how.

“I need *your* help.”

Chapter Three

Dork.

Daniel stood with his back to Zoe, feeling dumber than a bag of particularly stupid hammers. The hot flush of shame was all too familiar from high school. He was surprised it felt just as bad a decade later.

But it was his own fault.

He'd come here to find the Avignon Quatrain and had instead behaved like an adolescent boy with his first grope. Bad enough that he'd forgotten the job at the first sight of desire in her eyes. That paled into insignificance next to the fact this was *Zoe*. Keeping his libido in check around her in high school had been nigh onto impossible—he'd wanted her so badly it had almost outranked breathing—but he'd done it because she deserved the very best from him. He'd always, *always* put his lust second to whatever happiness he could help her to have.

He cared about her so much it hurt.

Dork.

Of all the words that dropped from Zoe's gorgeous red lips, that one hit him the hardest. Pain skewered him, bend-him-over, cut-him-off-at-the-knees pain, expelled-breath-with-none-to-replace-it pain.

He didn't care what names other people called him. He'd long ago gotten past that.

But this was Zoe, and he was vulnerable.

This was why he hadn't tried to find her in all these years. Why, even after he'd honed his body to be as strong as his mind, he'd stayed away.

This intense pain, from so small a slight.

Then she said, "Daniel." And "I need your help." Her tight vocal cords told him this was important.

As it always had, that stopped him.

He turned back, carefully hiding his feelings behind an automatically blank face.

She'd never been a drama queen, and the faint lines marring her perfect forehead were enough to confirm she was desperately worried.

His pain didn't matter. It never had.

She needed that key.

The prophecy would have to wait. "All right. Show me where you had it last."

* * *

Relief flooded Zoe's veins like cool water. Daniel wasn't leaving her.

She'd hurt him just now. Without meaning to, but he had a right to walk out. They had no official tie, not beyond having been friends years ago, and even that had been tragically one-sided.

He had every right to turn around and walk out of her life forever.

Instead, he was letting her take advantage of his kindness. Again.

A pang of conscience made her wish he was selfish like other men. That he'd help her find the key, yes, but for himself, because he wanted the Queen of Heart's prize.

But this was *Daniel.* He'd never been nice-with-expectations, only nice. He helped because he was an upstanding, reliable guy, loyal and caring.

No matter how she'd treated him.

Shame heated the tips of her ears. She tugged up her bodice as if it could cover her wayward thoughts. She stood—and without thinking, presented her back, for him to handle the zipper. Like he was her brother, or a lady's maid.

Her whole face flamed, but he zipped without comment.

"Thanks." Regret and worry tangled inside her. "Let me show you where I've been, from the beginning."

He followed her out. "Are you sure you lost this key? Maybe it was stolen."

Stolen? The thief would take her parchment. Urgency clawed through any embarrassment. She dashed all the way to the ballroom back door, yanked it open, and shoved unheeding through the crowd of elegant men and women to the case.

The display case was still locked, the parchment inside. Relief weakened her knees. She fell back against the table, one hand to her breastbone, her heart thumping rapidly beneath.

Daniel stood in front of the case, staring at it with the intense concentration she remembered from high school. "The words," he said. "They're French."

"Yes." Drawing in a fortifying breath, she straightened from the table and began to look around her for the glint of the key. "It's a French parchment. From the sixteenth century."

* * *

Daniel stopped breathing. French. Sixteenth century.

Like Jean-Dion d'Avignon.

His breath returned, quick with excitement. Lady Luck had finally decided to smile on him, despite Halloween. He knew in his bones—this was the form the prophecy had taken. The Avignon Quatrain.

The four leading words, indicating *quatre* or four lines, confirmed it, though the full text of the prophecy was obviously hidden, invisible.

He'd been looking for the prophecy in hidden places when it was here in front, all along. He laughed at the irony.

Opening his third eye, he examined the document on the etheric. Witch's sight wasn't magic, per se, but it could reveal traces of magic.

Sure enough, the illuminated letters pulsed with royal power. A rush of triumph lit his veins.

Then he caught faint smoky bands running around the page. He frowned and peered closer.

Was there a geis on this?

Keeping his third eye open wide on the parchment, he touched a finger to his chest, where his wand lay hidden inside his inner breast pocket, then touched the display. Again, not using magic, simply triggering whatever that smoke was...

A spark snapped, making him jerk and startling her.

"Static electricity," he said to cover.

Inside, he snarled. The damned thing was booby trapped. A powerful spell lay on the parchment, an antitheft geis. Nobody magical could take it. Which meant the only way for him to obtain it?

The owner had to give it to him.

He asked Zoe, "This is a prize, you said? For what?"

She barely paused her frantic perusal of the table and floor around them, even lifting the table skirts. "Didn't your date explain? It's for whoever romances the Queen of Hearts best."

"My date? Ah." That was how she thought he'd gotten into the ball.

But the Queen of Hearts was the parchment's owner. He'd bet his entire fortune that said Queen was Zoe.

Zoe had to give the parchment to him.

Damn and blast. Halloween had had the last laugh, again. Beautiful and savvy as Zoe was, she was human.

If she'd been one of the magical types, a witch, familiar, or shifter, all he'd have to do was tell her about the true nature of the parchment and ask her to give it to him.

But humans could not know about magic. The Witches' Council was very definite about that.

Lethally definite.

One of the two reasons they'd send out the headsman. The other was the witch/shifter taboo. The Council got extra crawly about the magical types cross-pollinating as it were, afraid it'd lead to extraordinarily gifted, monomaniacal monsters bent on world domination.

They terminated intermagical couples with prejudice.

If he blurted to Zoe about spells and seers, best case scenario, she'd call the psych squad on him. Worse case, she'd get a visit from an Enforcer with a very sharp axe.

He drew a determined breath. Not telling her. Not when there was an alternative.

He'd have to romance the Queen of Hearts.

Under normal circumstances, it'd be easy. Win the parchment using every iota of charm and seduction he'd learned in the last decade? He'd ensure both he and the Queen were well-satisfied with their interlude.

But this was Zoe. If he romanced her and she found out he didn't really mean it, that he was only after her prize, she'd be hurt.

His heart sank at the thought. He'd rather risk the Council's wrath than risk that.

You'd rather risk her death?

The thought of one rich mahogany hair of hers being harmed made him boil with anger and despair.

Only one choice. Entice her to give up the damned prophecy before any harm could befall her. Hope she didn't find out. Hope against hope that only he paid the painful price.

He was about to close his third eye when he caught it—an afterglow of magic around the case. Someone had tried to open it.

Not just someone. Another witch. Daniel's whole body iced.

Another witch had tried to take the Avignon Quatrain.

* * *

Zoe straightened at the sudden storm darkening Daniel's gaze. Anxiety wicked into her. "Is something wrong?"

He didn't answer, goosing her anxiety higher. He only reached toward the case with both hands. She expected more snaps of static, but nothing happened as he ran his palms over the glass, scrutinizing the parchment inside it with a gaze that cut from his mask like a blue laser. A delicious tang wafted from him. She leaned toward him, breathing deep, drawing the scent into her lungs.

She knew that smell. Testosterone. It signaled a hunter. Male aggression. Sexy as hell.

And a relief. Testosterone took what it wanted. Whatever happened between them now, Daniel wouldn't be so heartbreakingly selfless.

"Let's start at the beginning." His words were quick, decisive. "When and where did you first get the key?"

That was Daniel, always thinking, as sexy now as it had been in high school.

"Here, a few minutes before the doors opened. My planner was supposed to secure the case, but she'd left the key in the lock by mistake. I locked up, took the key, and dropped it somewhere safe." She pointed to her cleavage.

His gaze followed her finger, so fast his eyes nearly snapped off.

Her spirits buoyed, until she realized why.

Bitchslap me with a full moon. Helpful and selfless, *bad* qualities? Leering, *good*?

Daniel glanced at her with a quirked brow, as if asking *What's wrong?*

Zoe's face flamed, and she shook her head. Nothing was wrong except the shallow idiot she'd been in high school had made an encore appearance. *Please don't ask.*

Answering her unspoken plea as he always had, he simply went on. "All right. What happened then?"

"Well...I was on the phone with my cousin while I double-checked everything was in place for the arriving guests..."

Too late, she realized babbling about the key and *her* event planner would clue in a smart guy that she was the party's hostess, the Queen of Hearts. Daniel was *very* smart.

She was cudgeling her brain for a way to distract him when the accident happened. At first she was *grateful.*

A thud. A woman's, "*Oof.*" A clang-clatter, like something falling to the floor.

Then a beautiful woman stumbled against Daniel. He automatically reached out to steady her.

Grateful went poof. Zoe's wolf growled, not liking Daniel's hands on anyone but her.

She shushed it. He was just being nice. Helpful.

A young man in wait staff uniform stood frozen behind the woman, the fallen tray and the chagrin on his face telling the story of what had happened. "M-miss! I'm so sorry. I didn't see you." He snatched up his tray and began picking up tidbits of food.

"No harm done. Thanks to this *hero*." The woman leaned into Daniel, beaming up at him. She had the face of an angel, an hourglass figure sheathed in white silk, and she dripped so much money and class it made Zoe feel like she wore a leopard-print lampshade with cheap fringe.

Another growl buzzed Zoe's throat, not just her wolf this time. She cut it off, but it took more effort.

"Thank you," Miss Money Bags simpered at Daniel, batting her outrageously long lashes.

He gave her a distracted smile. "My pleasure."

Just being friendly. No reason to get jealous—

"Shall we find somewhere nice and quiet?" The woman threaded arms through his and tugged. "Where I can thank you more thoroughly?"

Mine.

Heat *fooshed* through Zoe. Instinct propelled her, rocket-like, between them.

The woman fell back, startled.

"Excuse me." Zoe raised her upper lip in a grin at the woman that was less smile, more wolf. Her canines may have even lengthened.

Miss Classypants paled. Releasing Daniel, she edged away then turned and scurried off.

Zoe turned to find Daniel frowning at her.

Crap on a claw. Humans didn't know about shifters, but that didn't mean they couldn't sense when things were weird. And Daniel, as she'd already remembered, was quicker than most.

Immediate distraction was in order.

"Where were we? Oh, yes, checking out the ballroom." She hurried toward the hors d'oeuvre table. After a moment, Daniel followed. She went on,

"I met a man in a ripped leather mask calling himself Zeus—a handsy sort." She touched her throat, remembering. "Then that sashed-up jerk caused a ruckus."

"Did he bother you?" His frown changed, darkening with anger.

"You were there. You saw me handle it."

"Not Lord Boozer. Zeus."

"Oh. No. Not much. I bet the key is just lost. It's crowded in here, and the key could have gotten bumped out by someone knocking into me."

Daniel shook his head. "You'd have heard it. What isn't hardwood dance floor is thin carpet over concrete, and your hearing is extraordinary."

Zoe's breath froze. Did he know she was a wolf? "What are you implying?"

"Not implying."

The only thing that stopped her heart from seizing was the fact that he headed back toward the parchment case. There, he spun to face her. "This handsy Zeus—how handsy was he with you? Tell me the truth, Zoe."

"Well, he..." She touched her cleavage, remembering his spelunking hand. "Oh, no."

"Oh, yes. Point Zeus out to me."

Her gaze flew up to Daniel, her heart beating faster. The thunderclouds in his eyes were darker than the mask that limned them.

Then he added, "His touching you is suspicious."

Investigating the key. Not...not whatever she'd thought. Which hopefully wasn't some cave-wolfie idea that he should fight for her.

"But Daniel, the parchment is still here. Why would Zeus steal the key but not use it?"

"That case is front and center. People pass it constantly. He can't unlock the case and take the parchment without being seen." Daniel's gaze on the prize was as sharp and concentrated as a hawk. Definitely not selfless, nor even brotherly.

She shivered, revising her estimate of him. "So he'll, what, cut the lights? Blind everyone with a smoke bomb?"

"Or he's planned a getaway and is simply waiting for the right time. Zoe. Point Zeus out."

His tone was as commanding as Noah's alpha bark. Automatically, she searched the ballroom for the brutal-faced man and his cowl.

She caught sight of him by the crèmes, cakes, and parfait table, squat but powerful, his shoulders twice as broad as any of the men and his grimace four times as mean.

A sudden fear stabbed her belly. Daniel thought Zeus had the key, and he was in fight mode. But in a fight, she wasn't sure the bruiser Zeus wouldn't beat Daniel to hell.

She turned to him, anxiety gnawing a hole in her. "I'll point him out in a second. But Daniel, how are you going to get the key?" She dared take his arm. "I don't want you confronting him."

He stared down at her for seconds that stretched. "You're worried about me?"

Heat rose up her neck. If he only knew how much.

* * *

Daniel searched Zoe's beautiful spring-green eyes and read her gnawing anxiety. *For me?* It amazed him.

She cared about him.

It shouldn't have mattered. But it did. He felt as if for years he'd been panting smog and suddenly his lungs were filled with clean oxygen.

It made his job more difficult, though. He'd known romancing her for his own ends would hurt her. But if her feelings were truly engaged, she wouldn't just be hurt.

She'd be hurt deeply.

He simply couldn't do it. He couldn't romance her for the prophecy. He'd have to try something, anything else.

Well. If he couldn't win her parchment through love, maybe win it through deed? Yes, he'd get her what she wanted most—the key.

He'd have done it anyway, but now it was twice as important.

Fortunately, it was an easy task. He was ninety-nine percent sure Zeus had stolen the key from Zoe's cleavage, and a hundred percent sure he'd knock the man into next week for treating her like that.

"I promise not to confront him unless there's no other choice. Now point him out to me, Zoe."

* * *

Zoe sighed, hoping she was doing the right thing. "That's him. The man in the ripped mask." She pointed at the crush of people around the cakes table—and realized Zeus was gone. "Well, he *was* there—"

"Look *out.*"

Slam. Splash. Something hit her outstretched arm.

She registered cold and sticky as liquid soaked into her bodice. A startled glance down showed her bosom unhappily rumpled. Her pointing finger curled, almost wilted. Her gaze flicked up.

Reeling back from her was the lecher she'd tossed out, the sashed-up marquessy guy. *How'd the jerk get back inside?* His stick-mask dangled from its ribbon, forgotten, as he stared into his empty glass, empty because his drink was now all over her—a thousand dollar drink, if his glare was any indication.

"Watch where you're pointing next time." He turned up his snout then turned to walk away.

"*Me?*" She wanted to kick his ass for real this time, but with Daniel watching, having just seen him behave so graciously with the gorgeous *classy* woman, Zoe could only fume impotently.

But then *Daniel* grabbed the man's shoulder and spun him. "Apologize to the lady."

"*Lady?*" The marquessy guy raised his mask-on-a-stick to sneer through it...at Daniel's tie. Daniel was just that tall. Lord Sash adjusted his sneer upward. "Puh-lease. In that ten-dollar dress?"

Daniel's eyes narrowed like blue sabers. "Apologize—twice. *Now.*"

Zoe recognized the deadly danger in that masked glare. While Daniel could easily take Lord Sash, and her wolf approved, a fight would spoil the ball's classy atmosphere. "My Hero, let it go. The Queen of Hearts will see this guy for the ass he is. He won't get the prize."

"If you think that's all I care about..." Daniel turned a hooded gaze on her. "You're mistaken, Lady Mystery."

In her periphery, the marquessy jerk started to slink away.

Without even looking, Daniel's hand shot out and he grabbed the man again. "We're not done."

"W-wait," the guy blubbered. "Look at her goose bumps. Don't you want to do something about it?" As he pointed at Zoe's breasts, a grin fluttered onto his face. "Abou-tit. Get it? Tit."

Zoe rolled her eyes. Howling moon, Lord Sash was either too drunk to care or a compulsive asshole.

Daniel ripped, "*Shut* it." Without releasing the guy, he snatched a napkin off a passing waiter's tray and handed it to her. "Lady Mystery. For your décolletage."

He'd solved her problem with brains. Her wolf grumbled that an alpha would've punched out the snooty guy's lights, but her human side was grateful.

She dabbed, torn, and uncomfortable about being torn. "Thank you, My Hero."

"Now apologize," Daniel said to the marquess.

"Sorry."

M'lord Sash really did look sorry, and for a moment Zoe was inclined to feel more charitably toward him.

Then he brightened. "In fact, let me make it up to you. I can do that." He snatched the napkin from her hand. As she stood there, surprised, he began swabbing her cleavage so enthusiastically her breasts looked like a two-ball Newton's Cradle and nearby people stopped to gape.

Zoe swatted the man's hand away. "Stop that."

"Whoa mama. Are these real?"

Before her wolf could throw the guy against the wall—and horrify her rich, elegant guests—Daniel caught the man's wrists in a handcuff hold. The tang of testosterone filled the air in luscious waves.

"You're done here." Jaw jutting, shoulders flared, Daniel dragged the marquess toward the front entrance. All the man's struggles and digging in of heels didn't even slow him down.

"My Hero." Zoe followed Daniel in wonder, sure her eyes in her mask were as big as saucers. Both her wolf and her human were thoroughly impressed. This was definitely not the high school weakling she'd known.

Her "aw, cute and loyal" burst. This was a dark, dangerous alpha of a man, and she suddenly hungered for him, so much so that she wanted to wrap her legs around his hips and beat against him until her thighs were slick and the ache inside her had eased.

Do it. See if he's the one. Deep inside, her wolf howled. *Try to* mate *with him.*

Insanely, as he shoved Lord Sash out the door, she opened her mouth to say it. *Let's go back to the prep room and lock the door...*

"Yes." Daniel turned to her, napkin in hand, eyes intense.

She thought he'd read her mind for a moment. That he wanted to prove himself her mate. Excitement surged in her breast.

Then he said, "I know how to find the key."

Chapter Four

Daniel, after kicking the marquess out, turned to Zoe, napkin in hand. "I have an idea. How to get the key."

Confusion crossed her face, and strangely, disappointment. But it cleared in a flash to determination. "What do you need from me?"

She didn't ask, "What are you going to do" or "How are you going to do it?" She simply trusted him to get the job done. As she always had.

His heart filled with emotion, a smile lifting his lips. Whatever else had changed, they still had this.

"I need you to guard the parchment case in case Zeus decides to use the key." He knew she'd be safe in a room full of people. "I'll need a room by myself to work things out. That empty prep room. Does the door lock?"

"Yes." Her cheeks colored momentarily, maybe remembering what they'd done there. What more they might have done. Daniel couldn't help remembering, himself.

"Perfect."

He escorted her to the case then strode from the ballroom into the cooler hallway. On the way to the prep room, he couldn't help pressing the napkin to his face. It smelled of jasmine and saffron perfume, the spilled drink, and that essential soft feminine scent that was Zoe herself. A deep shiver wracked him.

He put aside his own desires to attend to her needs, as he'd always done. *The key*. The Quatrain was protected against magical theft, but if Zeus was a mundane, he could steal the parchment. Daniel had to assume Zeus had the key and was just waiting for an opportune time.

So. Do the spell, find Zeus, punch out his lights for mauling Zoe, and take the key.

If Daniel was lucky, he'd have this whole thing wrapped up in fifteen minutes.

A basic Locate Object spell was one of the first lessons taught to a young witch or wizard. It wouldn't find Zeus, a Find-type spell that only worked for inanimate objects, but Daniel strongly suspected he only had to find the key to find the man.

Locater spells could get complex. They were like map directions, and the more you asked of the spell, the more difficult it got. But this one only had a starting point and an endpoint.

The key's starting point—Zoe's delectable bosom. Or rather, its representation. He lifted the cloth napkin to his nose. Sweet scent filled his nostrils, but it was more than a sachet. It was exactly what he needed to find the key.

First, water. Then a cauldron. Add fire, magic and stir. T-minus fifteen minutes to a satisfying punch in Zeus' face.

Tucking the napkin into his tux pocket, he returned to the hallway. The scent of roasted meat came from his right. He followed his nose to the food staging area where three people in white chef's coats flew in and out with dishes.

A young woman was wiping out an empty chafing dish. He asked her for water. She set down the dish, grabbed a carafe, and filled it from the tap. Handing it to him with a hurried smile, she grabbed a full tray of bacon-wrapped scallops and sailed out with it. A man carrying a foil pan sped out behind her, the savory smell of beef trailing him.

Daniel pretended to get a text message, fumbling with his phone while he watched the last caterer from the corner of his eye. The instant her back was turned, he snatched a canned heat, the empty chafing dish, his carafe, and left.

Daniel sped with his supplies to the privacy of the decorating prep room where he locked the door. He couldn't chance a human seeing him work magic. Best case scenario, he'd have to pay a stiff fine. Worst, Enforcers would come and strip him of all his powers—or his head. The Witches' Council took mundanes witnessing magic very seriously indeed, because if too many regulars knew about it, magic would cease to exist.

Like Schrödinger's cat, magical uncertainty, directly observed, collapsed into mundane reality. So magic was a secret, rarely done in front of mundanes and never in a way that they'd think it real. The Council even got crawly if shifters got involved, and they were magical beings. Then punishment depended on who heard the case and how paranoid he or she was. Imprisonment, heavy fines, stripped of his powers and, well, the Council did have that headsman on payroll.

With the door securely locked, Daniel did a quick etheric scan for electrical and metaphysical bugs. The room was clean.

Setting his materials on a table, he ticked them off against his mental list. Cauldron, water, fire, check.

Witches were able to manipulate the unknown that was magic without changing the essential uncertainty, but no one knew how or why. Certain ingredients, words, or ritual helped that manipulation, but again, no one knew why. Well, not since the metaphysical research branch was shut down centuries ago by the Inquisition. Some spells required a host of exotic ingredients, intricate words, or elaborate ritual.

Not this one. He poured the water into the chafing dish then lit the canned heat and placed it under the dish. Squaring his shoulders, he put the napkin in the water.

Daniel plucked his wand, ebony with gold wire fittings, from his breast pocket. The wand was always at hand when needed and never there to spoil the line of his clothes when he needed that. A wizard thing.

He poked the cloth with his wand until it was submerged then paused.

Locate Object was a heart spell. There was one exotic ingredient.

Blood.

Daniel couldn't keep dismay from chilling him. As a wizard prince he was master of several forms of magic. But the one aspect he could never seem to get was heart. Not since high school...he frowned. He was decent at it in high school. What had changed? Besides bulking up and actually getting dates, which should have increased his ability to do heart.

What had changed didn't matter. Even he couldn't screw up this simplest of Finds.

With a deep inhale, he took a sterile lancet packet from his breast pocket. As a wizard, he always had several.

Next, he used the lancet to prick his finger.

His blood gathered in a ruby tear, dangling from the pad. *Heart*. It dripped, fell into the water and dispersed. He tried not to think of Zoe as the second drop gathered.

Then it struck him—*that* was what had changed since high school.

His breath froze. The drop fell in silence. A single woman, affecting his magic? The blood hit the water and burst with a dazzle.

He didn't have time to deal with the implications. An excuse, but with the advantage of being true. It was a relief when the third drop finally fell, and he could press his thumb against the puncture to stop the bleeding.

Using the wand, he stirred the water three times. Then, with a flick of his wrist, he drew the blue flame onto the wand. Successive flicks wrapped it around the wand like cotton candy on a stick.

A fling sailed an arc of blue fire into the air and down into the pan.

Napkin, water, and blood all lit with a *foomph*. He mentally touched his power then spoke a single catalyst word.

"Find."

The flames began to dance and swirl, ghostly waltzers on a ballroom floor as the spell mapped a 3D hall onto the dish.

One spot pulsed red in the back of the pan, the back of the ballroom.

The swirling blue flame coalesced into that spot, like water spiraling down a drain. It flared orange-red and formed a brutal face in a ripped mask. The handsy Zeus had the key. Daniel's blood surged with triumph.

Then the fire spat flares of purple—and the flames turned totally black.

Black fire.

Stars and moon. This was a disaster. *Zeus is a witch.*

A find spell was a two-way street. Even a half-competent witch would feel it and could traced the spell back to Daniel.

He tore off his tux jacket and smashed it over the pan, smothering the magefire. His chest was pumping like a bellows.

Once the spell was doused, Daniel himself was essentially invisible, magically. Although power betrayed itself in certain signs, especially in the eyes, magic could only be sensed in action or on things, not in witches. The spell's trail on the etheric would lead to this room, but Daniel would be long gone. And as a witch, Zeus couldn't steal the Quatrain.

But none of that mattered now.

Black flames. Evil intent.

Zeus had plucked the key from Zoe's lovely bosom to steal the Quatrain. Stopped by the geis, his next move would be to try to get around it the same way Daniel was—manipulate the parchment's owner to give up the document.

Manipulate *Zoe* to give up the parchment.

The good news was, the geis wouldn't work under coercion, so he'd try persuasion first. Maybe even try to romance Zoe, the very thing she wanted.

But the instant Daniel had done his spell, Zeus would know another witch was onto him. He'd step up his schedule, rush Zoe to give up the parchment.

Maybe even try to force her.

Black flames. Evil intent. Daniel shuddered with rage at the thought.

He snatched up his jacket and, despite the half-charred lining, threw it on as he ran out of the room. Heart pounding, he raced for the ballroom. Zeus, an evil wizard, knew he'd been found out, and the clock was ticking.

Zoe was in danger.

Chapter Five

The moment Daniel left Zoe to guard the parchment case, she saw people glancing at the assembled orchestra.

She swore mentally. *Time to start the ball.* Normally as hostess, she'd have led the first waltz. But until her identity was revealed at midnight, the Queen of Hearts had to remain masked.

She left her guard duty for all of a minute to have a discreet word with the orchestra director.

As she was finishing her instructions, her wolf growled. She spun.

Headed straight for the case, unmistakable in his ripped-leather mask, was the handsy Zeus.

By her paws and claws. He'd light-fingered her key, and now he had the nerve to try to steal her parchment under her nose? Her wolf's growl deepened. *It* wanted immediate revenge, of the bloodiest kind.

But her human counseled caution. She didn't want to make a scene in front of her elegant guests. What to do?

Steal the key back.

Her blood lit with a fire. *Payback, you brutal bastard*. Then if that didn't work she'd let her wolf have its confrontation.

As the first strains of the "Blue Danube" began, she dashed to intercept him at the corner buffet table, full of cheese and chatting couples. Let Zeus try his shenanigans when she was ready for him.

He turned to her, a smile twisting his lips but a thunderstorm in his eyes. "Lady Mystery, there you are," he rasped. "Kismet brings us together again."

"Or your clumsy attempts to steal from me," she murmured.

"What?" he asked sharply.

"Nothing." She smiled coyly and fluttered her eyelashes at him.

Her wolf snorted in disgust, but her flirting must have appeased him because he relaxed.

"I was looking for you, darling. Where were you?"

"Me? I was outside, casing...I mean, strolling the gardens."

More like hiding, no doubt. She gestured at the table. "Cheese?"

"I have a better idea. Let's go somewhere we can get romantic." He clapped a hand on her shoulder.

She staggered, but kept her smile plastered on her face. "But darling." Fluttering her eyelashes like a power fan, she yanked loose. "Nothing is more romantic than cheese."

"Being alone together is. C'mon."

Zeus grabbed her wrist and tried to tug her toward the side service door.

She had no idea what he wanted from her, since he had the key, but the angry reek coming off him dumped ice into her veins. She resisted—and still got dragged a few inches. She had to let her wolf out to add strength.

On the plus side, she broke loose.

Huge minus, he glared suspiciously at her.

Damn it. She had to derail those suspicions, fast.

"Me, I love cheese." She pointed at herself, letting her finger sink into her cleavage.

His gaze shot down and widened.

Gotcha. As he licked his lips, Zoe backed toward the cheese table, widening the gap between them. *And for my next trick...* "I especially love Camembert, don't you?" With a flirty smile, she groped on the table behind her for a plastic sword pick. Her hand landed on one. For a moment, she considered using it on him.

But there was still the barest chance of getting the key back without disrupting her party. Instead, she stabbed a cube of cheese, hard.

His gaze rose, and he frowned. "I don't want cheese. I want to be with you—alone." He took a threatening step closer.

Falling back, she hit the table and gave a shocked little jerk. She covered by swinging the sword pick between them. "But the cheese is so creamy." Bringing the sword to her mouth, she licked the cube, slowly. Sensuously.

Zeus' expression changed, gaze riveted to her caressing tongue, his own emerging from between his lips as if mimicking her.

Her wolf snorted in disgust, but she counted it a win and let her wary muscles ease.

Until Daniel, nostrils flared like a bull, charged into the room.

* * *

Daniel rushed into the ballroom, head and stomach churning, gaze cutting left-right, frantic to catch a glimpse of Zoe.

The ballroom was filled with swirling dancers and chattering groups. He couldn't see the one lush figure he wanted. His heart thudded painfully. Damn it, a wizard was pursuing Zoe with evil intent, and Daniel had no idea where she was. Couldn't protect her, as everything inside him screamed to do.

As if Zoe was his to protect.

He ground his teeth. She wasn't his, she never had been. Despite what happened tonight on that fainting couch, he'd never rise to more than a friend.

Didn't stop him from wanting to protect her with every fiber of his being.

A gap opened in the crowd. Immediately he saw the ripped leather mask. *Zeus*. The mage's face was pinched in a brutal frown directed at a woman. A graceful woman with a river of dark, glossy hair.

Zeus is with Zoe. Daniel's heart stopped.

Then his pulse kick-started to pound twice as fast. To hell with whose she was or wasn't, he was going to rip Zeus apart.

Daniel bulled like a linebacker through the dancers. Urgency knifed him to simply mow them all down. He barely stopped himself from blasting them away with his wand.

If Zeus hurt her, he was a dead man.

As Daniel neared, he saw Zeus staring at Zoe, lust blazing alongside the cruelty in the man's eyes.

And Zoe... Daniel slowed as his whole body turned to rubber.

Her tongue curled around an hors d'oeuvre with such erotic heat, Daniel wanted to be reincarnated as that cube of cheese. Zeus leaned forward, for all the world like he was going to replace the cheese with his mouth.

Daniel's sight went red.

He sprinted for her, his conscience screaming at him to stop, that she deserved better than him, but he could care less; she was *his*, and no dollar's worth of wizard was getting in his way—

"Whoa there, cowboy."

A hand seized his shoulder and swung him around. He was confronted by a man in black tails and a satin domino styled to look like purple smoke. The man's lounging stance was graceful as a wild animal, but his smirk was all-too human.

Daniel twisted, trying to wrench away. "*Let go.*"

The man's fingers were steel. "I will, when you calm down." A touch of sympathy lit the amused black eyes twinkling through the domino.

"Right. All right." Daniel stopped tugging, pretending to cooperate, but he dragged oxygen rapidly through flared nostrils, ready for his opportunity to yank away. Maybe smash the man in the face as he did. No, that would take too much time, and he had to get to Zoe. "Who are you?"

The man's mouth quirked. "I've had many names. Currently, I'm going by the amusing sobriquet of

Jayden. I'm not letting you go, you know. What you're contemplating is a death sentence."

"How do you know what I'm contemplating?"

"Please." Black eyes rolled. "Your gaze on her is so hot you're about to trigger the sprinklers. You want to have steamy, meaningless sex with her. But I can tell you, intimacy between you two will be neither meaningless nor mere sex." He paused as if considering. "It *will* be steamy, though."

Smartass. "My intentions are none of your business."

"Normally I'd agree. In this case, I need to remind you witch/shifter mating is forbidden. On pain of death."

"How...?" The man knew Daniel was a wizard? Impossible. But even that paled compared to the thought that this Jayden might be a danger to Zoe. "Whoever your are, you're mistaken. Lady Mystery isn't a shifter."

"Isn't she? Take a look on the etheric."

Daniel blew out a hiss of frustration. "If it'll get you to release me faster, fine." He turned to Zoe, tried to ignore the way her luscious lips pursed around the tidbit of cheese, and opened his third eye on her.

Magic sparkled in her aura.

Wild. Animal. *Magic*.

He clamped his etheric eye shut. It couldn't be.

Of course it could. He wouldn't have known the signs in high school. But he knew now, from his arcane classes at Nostradamus University. He peeked again with his third eye.

Clamped all his eyes shut in frustration.

Damn it, Zoe Blackwood was a *shifter*. Wolf, if he read the signs right.

Things had just got a whole lot worse.

He'd only kissed her and briefly held heaven in his hands, but he wanted her with a hunger that poured off him. Sex with a shifter was taboo, enforced by the Witches' Council. Penalty of death.

And Jayden knew.

Fear for Zoe spiked Daniel's gut. "If you're a Council Enforcer—"

"Heaven forbid." The man's black eyes widened, and he briefly raised his free palm. "I'm just a friend."

"Well, *friend*, I don't take well to threats. Who are you, where have you come from, and what the hell do you want?"

"A guest, in the area like you, and to give you some advice." Steely fingers dug in so hard they nearly pierced Daniel's triceps. "You're not the only agent of prophecy here, so listen up."

Pain and surprise forced Daniel to obey, at least for the moment. "I'm listening."

"A wizard prince and the daughter of an alpha once got away with mating. Lived together, right under the Council's noses. Want to know how?"

Hell yeah, he wanted to know. But he only said, "What you're saying is impossible."

"Not impossible, simply very difficult. The wizard pretended the shewolf was his live-in housekeeper. Now, I'm not recommending that, because they were always looking over their shoulder and could never be themselves. No spontaneous displays of affection—no displays of affection at all, except behind locked doors with all the curtains drawn. Plus, no insurance benefits for her or the pup. How annoying is that? But they were able to live together without the Council knowing. They even had the kid."

"Lovely. I'll keep that in mind, if I ever decide to get serious with a shifter...damn." Daniel was speaking to thin air. The stranger Jayden was gone as if he'd never been.

A projection? But astral projections were tremendous power sucks, especially with a grip like that.

The whole bizarre incident, however, had taken precious moments.

Zeus, that slime, grabbed Zoe's wrists.

Fury surged in Daniel's veins. He plunged through the last of the crowd that separated them. Zoe wouldn't know Zeus was a wizard. Witches could recognize shifters, but though shifters knew about witches, they couldn't distinguish one from a mundane.

Zoe wouldn't know he was rescuing her from an evil wizard.

So last-minute, instead of cleaning Zeus' clock, he only made a hairpin of his arms, thrust them through Zeus', and broke the man's hold on Zoe with a quick twist.

Then Daniel snared Zoe's hands for himself and poured on the charm.

"Lady Mystery." He tossed her cheese onto the table and lingeringly kissed her fingers. "I was looking for you."

She frowned. "I'm *busy*." She added a mouthed, *Getting the key*.

So she wasn't actually interested in Zeus, she was just leading him along. He'd have been relieved, but she had no idea how dangerous Zeus was.

She had no idea Zeus wanted a new key to the parchment—Zoe herself.

Daniel adopted his best suave, seductive smile. "This will only take a minute. Zeus, is it?" He spun the smile into an insolent slap of a grin at the other wizard. "You don't mind if I steal this lovely lady, do you?"

"Yeah. I do." Lightning practically jagged in Zeus' eyes.

No subtlety at all, this one.

Which gave Daniel an idea. Zoe wanted the key, and no need for subtlety? He'd steal it back *with magic*. Right here, right now. He'd cover his actions so bystanders wouldn't know, but Zeus wouldn't fail to figure out Daniel was his nemesis.

That would take Zeus' attention off Zoe, Daniel's main intent. Bonus, it'd shout loud and clear to the fucker that if Zeus wanted Zoe, he'd have to go through Daniel.

Both Zoe and Zeus were frowning at him—maybe because his hands and jaw were clamped so hard his teeth were powder and his fingers were knots.

He deliberately eased into a more casual stance. "I'm not giving you a choice. I'm cutting in."

Zoe began, "My Hero—"

"The hell you are," Zeus finished.

"Language." Daniel touched his wand, where he'd shoved it into his side pocket, and primed a simple pickpocket spell. A favorite for playing pranks at

University, Daniel learned the spell early and used it often, if only in self-defense.

Zoe crossed her arms and gave Daniel a narrow glare. “I’m fine here, with Zeus.”

“You’re really not.” The simplest form of pickpocket used direct touch as a bridge. All Daniel had to do was stay in contact long enough for the key to transfer.

“Zeus and I were having a nice chat.” Zoe frowned. She knew he was up to something, but she wouldn’t know what.

And frankly, Daniel was more worried about Zeus. The other witch might sense the spell before the transfer was complete—unless Daniel did something to distract him.

“Marvelous. We can all three have a nice chat together.” He smiled broadly and mentally triggered the spell.

As he gave the bastard a buddy slap on the back.

On one hand, it worked to perfection. The bridge initiated, without his new buddy catching on.

On the other hand, it backfired spectacularly. Daniel had only to stay in contact long enough. But thanks to Halloween, the chaotic nature of magic, his suppressed rage at Zeus, or simply Fate’s nasty sense of humor, his slap had the power of a punch.

Zeus staggered forward several steps.

Daniel tried to follow the motion, to keep in contact, but that was the moment Zoe punched a frustrated palm against his pectoral, pushing him back.

She snarled at them both, “That’s enough macho crap.” Her anger was practically a physical force.

It startled him. His power flowed and instant longer before he cut the spell.

Like electricity forced to jump, magic surged over the gap from Daniel's hand to Zeus' back with a *whoosh* of superheated air.

Zeus yelped as if he'd been singed. "*Hey*. What the hell are you doing?" He spun toward Daniel, shoulders hunched to charge.

"I said *enough*." Zoe wedged herself between them, her masked gaze cutting from one to the other. "I'm a person, not a piece of meat to be fought over."

"Sorry. I'm sorry." Daniel groaned mentally. He was very sorry he'd upset her, but he also knew that, without the key, she'd be determined to stick with Zeus.

A determined Zoe was as stubborn as a cliff.

He'd have to confront the guy.

No, he couldn't. Magical fights between two witches, especially when it involved throwing raw power, could get messy. He couldn't chance her or anyone else getting caught in the crossfire.

He needed to get His Lady Stubborn away from Zeus. He didn't want her anywhere near the jackass.

But how?

The orchestra began another waltz. It gave him an idea. She'd planned this evening around the idea of romance? *He'd* spent the years since high school honing his seductive skills.

He took her fingers and kissed them. "Lovely Lady Mystery..."

He meant to follow up with, *Would you care to dance?* But his nose delighted in her unique scent, his lips tingled at the feel of her smooth skin, and all he wanted to do was kiss up her delicate hand, trace the veins along the back with his tongue, press hot lips to the inside of her wrist and kiss all the way up her tender inner arm to her sweet, hot mouth...

Need seared him, a fierce desire that raged almost immediately into direct action. Using his hold on her hand, he spun her into his arms and bent to seize her mouth.

Her eyes closed and her whole body softened in his arms.

His body fired up in response. Forget the key, forget the damned Quatrain. He started to sweep her up into his arms for a thorough kissing. To carry her to the prep room for a helluva lot more.

Zeus barked a protest.

The sharp sound called Daniel back from the brink of insanity. Zoe's responsiveness didn't mean she'd appreciate being mauled in front of her guests. He barely managed to turn the kiss into a press of lips to her cheek, just below her mask.

"Lovely Lady Mystery," he purred. "Come away with me."

She gave a throttled groan. "I want to. But..." Her lids rose. "I know you're trying to sidetrack me from Zeus."

"This chump? You don't want him. He's as romantic as a two-by-four." He searched her eyes, trying to tell her he was doing this for her own good, that the fire witch was dangerous. He'd have said the words, but with the creep right there, that would only put her in more peril. Instead, he said "You don't want this jerk—"

"Zeus." She stiffened in his arms, her chin kicking up. "His name is Zeus, and I'm enjoying his company. Let me make this plain, My Hero. *Go away.*"

Go away. Her words, so like so many others in high school, unexpectedly knifed his heart.

Daniel released her instantly. He knew she wasn't rejecting him, just trying to dazzle Zeus. Yet memory taunted, *go away, go away...*

Why did it hurt?

He stared into her gorgeous, angry green eyes. As a youth, he'd been infatuated with Zoe. But that was the past. Now, he could have any woman as he wanted.

Why does it hurt this much?

The truth struck him with a brilliance that cut. He didn't want other women, and it wasn't a *past* infatuation.

His heart wanted Zoe—and it had only ever wanted Zoe.

Bright reality blinded him. Scared the crap out of him. After all the rejections in high school, he'd promised himself *no more pain*. Playing the field, he never got too close to anyone. The idea of settling on one woman, especially the one woman who mattered—who'd always mattered, the woman who could hurt him above all others?

Gut-wringing terror.

Zeus spoke into the silence, his gaze lit with cunning. "Lady Mystery. Let's you and me get out of here."

The words were for Zoe, but the brutal bastard was grinning at *Daniel*. And then, with two fingers,

Zeus slid a peek of something from his breast pocket. A mahogany curl.

A lock of Zoe's hair.

Daniel's heart stuttered in sheer terror.

Magical resonance. With that perfect curl, Daniel could set a romantic mood tuned just for her—and Zeus could enthrall her into doing his will.

Brutal eyes danced, gloating. *I can get the parchment from her whenever I want*, they said. *However I want.*

Daniel growled, low in his throat. His feelings didn't matter. The parchment didn't matter.

Blast subtlety. *Get Zoe away from Zeus*—now.

Daniel grabbed her wrist and tugged her toward the back doors.

Caught off guard, she got all of two feet before digging in her heels. Not stopping him, but slowing him.

He simply hauled harder.

She hissed. "Your caveman tactics don't impress me."

"I'm not trying to impress you," he hissed back. "I'm trying to rescue you."

He'd take her out of the ballroom, to the prep room. No, farther. Offsite altogether. He burned to drag her to a hotel where Zeus would never find her, and Daniel could ply her with drinks and kisses and plunder her...

"I can take care of myself." Her wrist tingled under his hand.

Magic.

She'd accessed her wolf to stop him. His heart hiccupped. She was serious.

He'd *never* force a woman.

Daniel stopped hauling. His hand sprang open, but his fingers lingered on her wrist because, even now, he couldn't keep from touching her. He spun to face her. "Not against this guy, you can't."

She searched his eyes. He let her read his concern for her, his entire focus on her green eyes, her very being—

"Let her go, asshole." Zeus slapped his palm into Daniel's shoulder, rocking him back.

"Make me." He muscled Zoe behind him. Part of him was aware he was behaving like a beast—specifically a wolf, challenging a rival to fight. Primitive and barbarous, not romantic and chivalrous at all.

But control and caution had all but abandoned him. He faced the evil fire witch with his chest heaving great gulps of oxygen. "Just try."

Zeus' jaw kicked out. "You think I won't?"

Daniel ripped a grin at the fire witch. "I'm hoping you will."

Zeus snarled in return. "Okay, tough guy, here it comes—"

"*Enough.*" Zoe stalked out from behind Daniel, glaring equally at him and Zeus. "What is wrong with you two? Are you trying to cause a scene? My Hero, I'm going with Zeus—"

"Wait." Not taking his eyes off the enemy witch, Daniel grabbed her shoulders and said the first thing he could think of to distract her.

"Marry me."

Chapter Six

In high school, Zoe had easy sex with boys who couldn't get enough. As a shifter, she couldn't get enough, either.

Until she met Tommy.

Captain of the football team and honor student, he'd had a great part-time job and a sweet motorcycle. He made her heart sing. Best of all, sex was awesome.

She'd thought he was "The One." The boy she'd spend the rest of her life with, the boy for her. He was human, but hell, she was young and didn't know all about mates, or even much of anything about them.

She'd given Tommy her girlish heart.

Then her period was late. Really late. Excited and scared, she told him that she thought she was pregnant, by him. That they were going to be parents.

She'd been excited. Happy.

He called her *dumb*. Said she was an *animal*, that she was the one who wanted all the wild sex, so she'd have to take the consequences.

Tommy dumped her then and there.

She was crushed. Sure, she'd been dumped a time or two before, but this was different. He was supposed to be *the one.*

He hadn't felt the same way. Or he was too scared by the responsibility. Either way, he'd bailed.

That night, Daniel had come over to her house to help her study, as he'd been doing for a few weeks. He'd made it his personal goal to help her pass chemistry class so she could get into college. She'd thought his persistence was cute.

Daniel had known instantly that something was off. She could tell by the considering way he looked at her. But he hadn't said anything, and she'd been grateful.

"So," he said. "How'd you do on the midterm?"

"Midterm?"

"Yes. Remember, the chem midterm you promised me you'd study for every night?"

"Well..."

She hadn't studied, not nearly enough. Because she'd wanted to be with Tommy, the boy she'd thought was *the one*, the boy who'd dumped her.

She'd flunked. But if she told Daniel that, he'd dump her faster than Tommy.

Somehow Daniel knew anyway.

"You didn't study, did you?"

She shook her head. "And I...I didn't pass." She cringed.

"I see." But instead of washing his hands of her, Daniel only nodded. *"Well, we all make mistakes. Do things we wish we'd done differently."* Then he hit her with those starburst eyes. *"What's wrong, Zoe? You can tell me. I won't judge you."*

She'd broken down and confessed. About Tommy dumping her. About maybe being pregnant. And Daniel...he studied her face, so seriously, so carefully...and said...

"Marry me."

The sweetest words. She'd wanted so much to hear them burst impulsively from *Tommy's* lips. She *had not* wanted them to come from a dork, especially since he'd had to think it over.

"You don't mean it," she said. "We don't love each other."

"We don't?" His gaze had shifted to her window, though he didn't seem to be looking out of it. Finally he nodded, and returned his eyes to hers. *"Tell me this. Do you want to pass your class? Honestly, Zoe?"*

The class had been all she had left. *"Yes."*

"Then I'll stick with you until we get it."

And he'd turned to the next chapter.

She'd been amazed and heartened that he hadn't abandoned her. Thinking she was pregnant, his proposal rejected, and yet he stayed with her. Yes, she wasn't pregnant, and yes, he hadn't meant his proposal, but her rejection still must've stung him.

Most importantly, he'd said *we*. Not, "I'll stick until you get this." But, "I'll stick until *we* get this."

Now, tonight, again, Daniel said, "*Marry me.*"

The sweetest words. She'd been waiting years to hear them burst impulsively from a man's lips.

No. She'd been waiting years to hear them burst impulsively from *Daniel's* lips.

But like this, so cold, so calculating...

Zoe stepped back as if struck. The blood drained from her, her body like ice. If he'd said, *I love you,* first, or even once looked at her... But his masked face was turned toward Zeus, his narrowed gaze locked with the other man.

The words were even more hollow than last time.

"You don't mean it," she whispered, voice hoarse.

The one boy who'd had no agenda beyond simply helping her was now a man who didn't care, like the rest.

Her heart shriveled in her chest.

But she was a wolf in the line of alphas and a business owner to boot. Daniel was only trying to distract her, from Zeus, from the key, it didn't matter. Resolve stiffened her spine, and she dropped her hand. *Stick to the original plan.* Find out where Zeus had the key. Get it back however she had to. Use the parchment to get a taste of romance.

And then get on with the rest of her barren-looking life.

* * *

Daniel was horrified when, at his impromptu proposal, Zoe's face turned white. He wished with all his might her green eyes would light with a stubborn glint. That she'd straighten her back and snap a "Not on your life" at him, no matter how badly that boded for him or cooperation.

He'd take a thousand glints over a single moment of shock.

Instead, she'd whispered, *"You don't mean it."*

If only she knew how wrong she was.

But then she turned to Zeus, held out her hand and said, "Let's find someplace private."

Daniel's lungs seized.

The ass sneered triumphantly at him, inviting a punch to the nose.

Zoe tapped a playful finger on Zeus' jaw to turn his attention to her. Curling a flirty come-hither finger at him, she sauntered off.

Daniel realized her game plan and wanted to howl. She thought she was going to take Zeus to the prep room and use seduction to get the key from him. Stun the brutal-faced mage with her gorgeous body.

But as stunning as her body was, with that mahogany curl, the witch could turn the tables on her in an instant.

Zeus could bewitch her, literally.

The thought turned Daniel's lungs to ash. He'd be damned if he'd let it get that far. Which meant getting the key *now*.

He bulled after Zoe, stopped her by grabbing her shoulders, and whirled her to face him. "I'm sorry, Lady Mystery. I got carried away by your beauty. Your feelings are not to be trifled with, and you're not an object." If he'd had time, he'd have separated his apology from what he was about to do. But speed was of the essence. "Though any man would be glad to fight for your *attention*."

On the word *attention*, he brushed his wand in its pocket, priming the spell. He was a wizard prince. If he couldn't make a magical touch bridge to retrieve the key, he'd make a purely magical one.

In his periphery, Zeus was scowling.

Daniel knew the mage had felt the shift in energies, but he was already a step ahead.

"I'm simply so glad I *found* you."

On the word "found" he pointed the primed finger at Zeus. The brutal-faced wizard's eyes widened. He pressed a hand to his belly, over his cummerbund.

So that was where he'd hidden the key. Didn't matter now.

"Found you *here.*" Daniel touched his finger to his unburned breast pocket and immediately felt the added weight of the key drag the inside lining down.

Zeus' hand clutched his cummerbund. "You stole it." The shock in his eyes as he dug at the black satin was almost comical.

"I certainly did. It's *golden.*"

Zeus' eyes in his ripped mask narrowed dangerously. He drove a hand into his jacket pocket. Summoning his wand no doubt, but it was far too late. *Golden* had locked the key in Daniel's pocket. Zeus couldn't steal it back, at least not via magic. Daniel gave the wizard a triumphant grin. Not as good as punching him in the nose, but he'd won.

Giddiness rushed hot in his veins. He had the key. The means to win Zoe's undivided attention and to earn the parchment was now in his grasp.

Zeus' next words chilled the victory.

"You think you've won. But I'll *make* her hand over the Quatrain." The brutal-faced mage turned to the nearest table and set a hand on a silver chafing dish.

The small flame wavered beneath it. *Fire.*

Zeus was going to cast a fire spell. He'd have to conceal it from mundanes or risk the Council's headsman, so it couldn't be too destructive.

Unless he was just that pissed off he didn't care.

For himself, Daniel could counter anything the bastard could throw. But if he wasn't fast enough to protect Zoe...

Heart thudding, he laced fingers through hers. "We have to get out of here."

She resisted. "The key—"

"I have it."

She gave him a shocked look, followed by a delighted laugh. "How do you do it? You're amazing. Okay, this way." She pulled him into motion, headed for the back of the ballroom. It was slow-going, wedging through the crush of guests munching beside the buffets and chatting in clumps, but Zeus wouldn't have it any easier following.

"You really pissed him off, getting the key," she said as she zig-zagged. "He wants to murder you."

"Not literally?"

"Yep. Or at least severely maim you." Her lustrous hair swayed as she barged around a knot of people admiring the parchment. "Believe me. I can smell it coming off him. Um, I mean *practically* smell it."

Daniel smiled. Her occasional odd language made sense, now that he knew she was a shifter.

His smile faded when he glanced back to see Zeus dodging after them, death in his eyes. It didn't take a shifter to read his intent—hurt Daniel, capture Zoe.

Which meant getting out of his line of fire as fast as possible.

"Where are we going?" Despite being chased by an evil wizard, Daniel liked the feel of Zoe's hand in his. Liked the wickedness of getting away with something together. This was almost fun.

As if she shared his delight, she tossed a grin over her shoulder. "You'll see. Damn, he's catching up. Can you do something to distract him?"

"A smoke screen? Sure." He glanced around. Witnesses here prevented him from smacking Zeus with pure power. But Daniel had combat magic training and knew how to use his environment. He knew several spells to nudge natural things to help him, with the mundanes none the wiser.

As Zoe turned front, Daniel touched his wand then swept a finger at a row of tea-candle-lit chafing dishes, muttering under his breath, "Smolder." Zeus was the fire witch, but as a wizard prince, Daniel had command of all the elements.

Smoke belched from the flames, charring the dishes' metal to black. The back of the room filled with a thick, billowing haze. The caterers scrambled for fire extinguishers, although the magical smoke would dissipate as soon as Zoe and Daniel were gone.

She flashed him a startled glance. "Wow. When you say smoke screen, you really mean it. How did you do that?"

"Umm...I didn't. Lucky coincidence."

He was saved from having to answer further when she pointed at a small, almost invisible doorway near the room's corner, not the one they'd used to get to the prep room.

"That's our way out..." She glanced over her shoulder. "Oh, no."

Daniel cut a glance behind. Zeus practically crowd-surfed through the smoke to lunge for them.

"Quick." Zoe sprinted and dodged the final yards for the door.

"I'll catch up." Daniel spun, braced, while his brain shuffled facts. Zeus was following them too closely for a clean escape. Delay him, then, but no overt magic, not with witnesses.

One option leaped to mind. *The fact I've been itching to do this?* Bonus.

He made a fist and, on an arm as rigid as a flag pole, raised it to Zeus' nose level.

Just as the evil wizard cleared the crowd.

Zeus's momentum drove his face into Daniel's knuckles. *Wham.*

The fire witch fell to his knees, hands clapping to his cowled face. Blood and curses ran freely from underneath.

Daniel's knuckles rang with pain. But damn, that had felt so good.

"Macho overcompensating hero."

He glanced behind him to see Zoe stopped beside the small door, arms folded, a half-amused, half-despairing expression on her face.

"Or idiot?" He shook his hand, shaking off the blow.

"Same thing." But her tone held an element of admiration.

"You were supposed to escape." He stalked toward her.

"*We're* supposed to escape. Come *on*." She grabbed his wrist and yanked him out the small side door.

Daniel found himself in a narrow, windowless corridor. A couple spooned against one wall.

"Where are we?" he asked.

"Old servants' passage. This way." Zoe pulled him faster.

They'd gone maybe fifty feet when the door slapped open behind them, accompanied by Zeus' roar. "*The woman is mine!*"

Now Daniel had a problem. Bare corridor meant no props he could use against Zeus. No crowd between them meant no cover. And with that couple as potential witnesses, he had to be cautious about using his power. Although, they didn't appear to be paying much attention. They'd barely looked up at the evil wizard's roar, maybe thinking it was part of some dramatic game Daniel, Zoe, and Zeus were playing.

Problem was, if the other witch was reckless enough, killing a few witnesses might be merely collateral damage.

What to do, what to do?

Burst all the lights? Darkness would hide his magic from the mortal couple. But again, slinging raw magic might hit innocent bystanders. Daniel couldn't chance it.

"We need to hide," he whispered to Zoe.

"Right. This way." She lunged to her right

Instantly she reared back, which shot his heart into his throat. But she was just opening a heavy metal door.

She ducked out, and he dived through after her.

Fresh air blew sweet and cool in his face. He was surprised to see they were in a private outdoor garden in the middle of the villa.

The courtyard was empty except for another couple making out. Hells bells, why couldn't people get their romance on *inside* the ballroom? Pulse racing, Daniel swept a quick recon. The foliage was mostly climbing vines and teacup bushes, useless for hiding. They were still vulnerable.

"No good." He urged her to keep moving. "We have to find somewhere completely hidden. Preferably with a locked door. Not the prep room." He'd done the find spell there. It was the first place Zeus would look.

"You don't ask for much, do you?" Her tone was light as she grasped his hand in a renewed hold and tugged him forward.

He ran behind her along the colonnade portico, head swiveling for entrances. Her wolf must've been to the fore, because she was almost too fast for him. His heart pounded as he tried to keep up, his breath rasping in his lungs.

Running faster than he'd run in his life, and it was almost not fast enough. They'd wheeled through a corner when the door banged open behind them.

Zeus shouted, "Give me that woman!"

What a one-trick pony, Daniel thought—just as power shot past his head and crashed into the stucco of the wall next to them.

"What the hell...?" Zoe growled the words as she whipped a quick glance back. Her wolf was definitely close to the surface.

Adrenaline kicked Daniel up beside her, to shield her if another blast came. Yeah, everyone knew magic was too touchy to improvise, and it was safer and less of a personal drain to cast tried-and-true spells or trigger imbued objects.

But in combat, a sprayed blast of raw power was as good as buckshot or a bomb.

"Hey," the guy in the kissing couple yelled. "Keep it down. You're spoiling the mood."

"There." Zoe tugged him toward an arched door directly opposite the ballroom. She sprinted for it.

Daniel admired Zoe's ability to run, especially considering she was in high heels.

Footsteps thudded through the garden, Zeus cutting a direct path.

Damn it. Daniel let go of Zoe's hand to stop and defend her while she got away.

Or he tried to. Her fingers tightened painfully around his, and she yanked him hard enough to get him airborne. "You're not pulling that again, Light."

And then they were at the door. Zoe practically ripped it open then dragged Daniel through.

He found himself in another hallway, this one all windows.

Hiding place. The corridor stretched for seeming miles. Nothing but windows. Nowhere to hide. No doors to lock. Muscles tightening, nerves singing, he swung his head left...and nearly missed the exit door directly across from him.

Zoe saw it at the same time. She flashed a grin at him, and despite the danger, the sun rose inside his heart. Renewing his grip on her hand, he dashed them through.

Onto the festively lit, upper lakeside terrace. Lake Michigan was a slash of gray-blue on the horizon.

The terrace was empty of people.

Yes. Free to use his power, Daniel now had a chance. Time to come clean about being a witch. He didn't know how much Zoe knew about magic—wolves knew about witches, but the two sets didn't exactly mingle—so he opened his mouth to prepare her for the mages' battle. "Zoe, I'm—" Catching sight of a set of security cameras scanning the patio, he groaned, "—screwed."

Behind them came the slap of a door and Zeus' muffled roar.

"Lower terrace?" she asked.

"Right behind you."

She flew across the patio, with him drafting in her wake. He was careful to keep his body between Zeus and her, braced for another blast of magic. If the fire witch was throwing raw power, he couldn't keep it up for long.

Even with the danger, running with Zoe, the wind in his face, her slim hand in his, paced in perfect synch, buoyed him, energized him. He hadn't been this alive, this happy, since high school.

Magic zinged past his ear, so close his hair singed.

"Stop, you bastard," Zeus bellowed. More power sang toward them.

Daniel threw up a quick shield, covering it for the cameras as a swipe to his forehead. He was surprised when the sleeve of his tux actually came away damp.

"He's persistent." Zoe started down the south set of elbow-bracket stairs.

The moment they turned onto the return flight, Daniel could see the open lower terrace wasn't any better for hiding, either themselves or his use of magic.

But across the terrace and a few more flights down was his car. "Zoe, my car. It's parked on Lincoln

Memorial. Right in front." Hopefully RD HOG hadn't come back and crumpled the Ferrari in revenge.

"Great." As they hit the last couple stairs, she raised her voice, almost shouting, "*Which car is yours?*"

"*Shh.* If he knows—"

"*Is it that red Ferrari?*"

"Damn it, Zoe—"

"Quiet." She yanked him to a stop on the lower terrace and faced him. "Not a peep, or I'll have your balls for my personal chewtoys, hear? Sorry if the Ferrari really is yours, by the way."

He opened his mouth to ask a pointed question or two, realized she had a plan, and shut it with a snap—then actually heard her words. *Her lush mouth on my groin...?* He swallowed, hard.

She nodded, satisfied, toed off her high heels, snatched them up, and led him cat-footed across the lower terrace. *Across,* not toward the razorback stairs down the bluff.

Toward the mirror staircase on the other side.

Zeus appeared at the top of the south stairs, his back to them as he started down.

Daniel's heart thumped, waiting for him to turn his head and see them, right out in the open.

Arrogant or in a hurry, the other mage didn't check to see where they were, or where they were headed.

We might actually get away with this.

While Zeus' back was turned, Daniel and Zoe slunk up the north staircase, Zoe monitoring the cowled wizard with glances cast over her shoulder.

Her shifter body-awareness no doubt kept her from tripping.

Just as the evil mage turned the stairs' bend, she dropped. She pulled Daniel down with her.

He crouched beside her in the shadows of the thick concrete spindles, holding his breath, pulse thumping madly. Waiting to be discovered.

Zeus plunged onto the terrace. Daniel's lungs began to ache.

The bastard stopped mid-terrace, head whirling like a hunter seeking prey. Burning to breathe, Daniel clenched Zoe's hand. She gripped his hard in return, reassuring him.

Finally, *finally,* the fire witch shouted, "The key and the woman are mine," dashed to the long switchback descending the bluff, and started down.

Daniel's breath whooshed out in relief.

Zoe tugged him to a crouching stand. "Come on," she hissed. "He's watching his feet. The minute he looks up, he'll see we're not on those stairs."

"Unless the lake creates an optical illusion." Daniel touched the wand in his pocket, pointed at Zeus and said, "He's following a *phantasm.*" On the word, a shadowy double blob appeared on the switchback, vaguely couple-shaped.

They crept up the stairs, keeping watch on the cowled wizard.

Suddenly Zeus looked up. Zoe froze, clutching Daniel's hand tight. Despite the furious rush of his blood, he liked that, liked the feel of her relying on him.

Zeus waved his fist—at the blob. "Give me back that key."

A spray of magic shot from his fist.

"What was *that?*" Zoe's eyes were wide. "Did he just shoot electricity from his bare hand?"

"Yes..." He almost added, *An evil witch is after you...* Yeah, that would potentially scare the crap out of her. If she wasn't thinking magic, now wasn't the time to tell her.

"Maybe some sort of freehand stunner." He urged her into motion again.

"That shoots electricity?"

"Um, yes?"

"Cool." Taking the lead, she ran him up the rest of the stairs.

On the upper terrace, he said, "When he finds my car empty, he'll come back. We need to hide."

Or at least go someplace where he could grab a breath, explain things to her, then go out to fight this fire witch alone.

She hauled him into the house, zipping along from one hallway into the next until it seemed as if they'd run all the way back to the ballroom, twice

Finally she found the janitor's closet.

She pushed him inside, crowding in behind him, and flipped on the light.

Daniel bent over and sucked oxygen. Panting, he tried to form words to explain. His image, opposite him in a mirror over a shallow floor basin, mimicked him. To his right was a rack of equipment, to his left a set of shelves. Behind him, Zoe shut and bolted the door.

She fell with her back against it, her chest pumping hard with sobbing noises.

She's crying. Explanations and heroically going off to fight the villain flew out of his head. He whirled to comfort her.

She raised her head, eyes brimming with tears behind her mask—cheeks and lips plumped with...a smile.

She was *laughing*.

"I can't believe that worked." She shook her head, thick lustrous hair swishing against the mounds of her breasts. Under the dress, the October chill had tightened her nipples into points. Zoe adopted Zeus' heavy growl. "Gimme the key and the woman!" She fell to laughing again.

Beautiful Zoe, laughing. It was magnetic, impossible to resist, and he joined in, feeling light.

"Classic villain, right?" He twirled imaginary mustache ends. "You must give me what I want—or else!"

"But I can't." Touching wrist to forehead, she affected a fainting heroine pose. "I can't pay the rent."

"But you must pay the rent. One way *or another*." With a lecherous grin, he waggled eyebrows, the mask tugging at his face.

Her own smile dissolved into something much more serious, much warmer. She tossed aside her shoes. "I'll take the other."

Gazing into her eyes, the moment bubbled inside him with infinite possibility. Anticipation lit his veins, his muscles, fueling his reaching for her. To his shocked delight, her arms lifted at the same moment, hands eagerly reaching for him.

She met him in an explosion of lips and tongues and groping hands. He was surprised their magic didn't ignite. More than a kiss, he devoured her and she him, merging mouths like mixing essences. He ran ardent hands over her curves. She was so soft, yet sleekly muscled.

Twining her arms around his neck, she pulled him into her, kissing him as if trying to crawl down his throat, so enthusiastically he laughed, "Wait."

"No more waiting." She peeled the jacket off his shoulders, continuing to dive into his mouth with abandon.

Ah, hell. This was wrong on so many levels, but everything he'd wanted, *dreamed* of, for years was within his grasp.

She was right. No more waiting. Daniel helped her get his jacket off then yanked open his bow tie and threw it away, just as it occurred to him that he could have done some interesting things with it.

She'd already flipped off his cufflinks and was busy popping the studs of his shirt, kissing and licking the corner of his mouth as she worked the small pearl-and-onyx fasteners free. Her tongue was hotter than a flame.

"How'd you get the key from him? I never saw it. You're amazing."

His chest swelled. "It wasn't hard. While he was busy with his posturing, I picked his pocket." As he reached behind her to unzip her dress, his lips found her tender earlobe. Kissing her soft flesh made his mouth buzz.

"Sneaky. Smart."

His chest expanded so much he had an insane urge to beat it like a silverback ape.

She undid the last of his studs and yanked the tail of his shirt from his pants, nearly ripping cotton. "At least you're not wearing one of those sash things."

"A cummerbund?"

"Man girdle. Yeah." When she frantically pushed apart his shirt and revealed his T-shirt, she released a groan. "Will these clothes never end?"

In answer, he grabbed the bottom of both shirt and T-shirt and tugged everything off over his head. His mask nearly came off with them. He couldn't quite care, except it left one eyehole off-center.

Her eyes roved over his naked chest. "You've bulked up since high school. It hasn't changed you."

The frank appreciation in her gaze made him hot, but her words didn't. "What do you mean, I haven't changed?" He'd changed plenty. He'd done the hard work to be worthy of her.

Zoe unzipped her dress—then stripped it off. Her breasts sprang free, and her navel was a perfect dent in her creamy belly. She stood before him in lacy panties, thigh highs, and nothing else. He gaped, stunned motionless except for his roving gaze.

He'd never be worthy of her. His heart fell.

As if confirming it, she said, "You're still a dork."

"Not anymore," he objected.

"Not any less," she retorted.

Then she grabbed him and kissed his astonished mouth so deep, it was as if she was mating it. Automatically, he wrapped arms around her slim, nearly naked body. Skin-to-skin, she stretched herself along him, her breasts crushing against him in her urgency.

His whole body lit on fire.

She petted his ribs and chest until he was broiling and eager to be completely naked, too. Naked with her in a janitor's closet. Not very romantic. Somehow, he couldn't quite care. Because, naked. With her. It was romantic enough for him.

"Is dork a good thing?" he asked hopefully.

"Are you still thinking?" she countered.

"Not much."

"Which means some." She glanced at his mask. "You're crooked."

"I know. I'm thinking, but only how to best please you."

She adjusted his mask with a smile. "Then you have your answer."

"I do?" He was confused and astonished and so aroused it was painful.

"My sweet dork." Zoe plastered both hands against his chest, pushing her bountiful breasts together like a harvest cornucopia. "If you weren't, you'd turn your brain off—and the only thing you'd care about was how to please *yourself*. But you're thinking about *my* desires."

Fierce satisfaction seared him. "Then I like dork."

"And so do I." She leaned in and took one hot lick of his chest.

His whole body clenched in anguished need.

Chapter Seven

Zoe had never tasted anything so good as Daniel Light.

Palms braced on his pecs, she leaned in and licked again. He was slick from their run, and her tongue skated over hard mounds of muscle and sleek hot skin, making her groan. "This has changed since high school. A lot."

He gasped a laugh. "How would you know? You never touched me like this then."

"I thought about it."

"You *did?*"

She peeked up. His shocked face would've been funny if she wasn't so hot for him. But she was, and his naked torso was even more ripped than a wolf's. Pressing herself against it, she was overcome with the need to kiss, lick, *bite* all that glorious male strength. She couldn't get enough of him.

Overcome with lust—and something more?

Whatever. He felt and tasted so good, nothing mattered beyond now. She petted everything she could reach as he caressed hard palms over her in return.

Each stroke aroused her more. His skin was hot silk over iron, his back broad wings of muscle that stretched and contracted as he caressed her. She grabbed those powerful wings. After a luscious grope or two, she slid her hands slid down to his narrow, muscled waist.

His mouth was on the crook of her neck, chasing hot shivers of desire along her skin. Lifting on her toes, she pressed into him, rubbing her nipples erect against the light hair of his chest. Need sparked through her breasts.

He slid his hands between them, down her belly, burrowing into her panties.

"Not yet." She stepped back, popping his hand out. Quickly, she reached in to work his zipper open.

"You first." Panting, he grabbed her wrists.

"No. Can't wait." She peeled his pants and boxers down a few inches then grabbed for him.

His cock sprang greedily into her hands, two fists' worth. She stroked the sleek, hard skin, and his fingers loosened and fell away.

"Okay...whatever you say. Whatever you want."

"Daniel, I want you to..." She gestured at him, his pants, and the door.

He read her flawlessly, as he always did. He shoved his clothes down to his feet and kicked them off then went to the door.

He leaned his back against the metal. His erection jutted eagerly toward her.

Oh, yes.

She sauntered toward him, stopping when the tip of that gorgeous cock brushed her belly. His breath sawed in and out, his eyes going supernova.

Giving him a devilish smile, her gaze never leaving his, she slowly knelt.

The rasp of his breath stopped.

Much better. She gave him a hot little lick.

A throttled noise came from the back of his throat, almost like a howl. So she had to, she really did.

Opening her mouth, she drew him in.

He hissed.

She sucked.

"You," he panted, pulling out. "You now."

The sight of him, full and straining for her, took her breath away. Made her heart pound double time. He was so tense, so ready, his muscles stood out like bricks.

Rising, she turned her back to him, hooked her panties with her thumbs, and drew them down her hips, teasingly slow. "How about nobody first. How about us, *together*?"

Daniel swallowed, hard. "Zoe, don't. I haven't...I didn't..."

She cocked a little smile over her shoulder. "No condom? That's okay. I'm good without." Wolf shifters were immune to most diseases and didn't have to worry about children until mated.

His breathing became rough. "Don't offer unless you really mean it—"

She tilted up her naked rump.

Instantly he seized her hips, fingers biting into her.

An excited gasp escaped her throat, anticipation soaring. Her sex throbbed for him.

Fingers clenching and unclenching, he panted hard, obviously still trying to restrain himself.

All that control. Sexy, but enough was enough. She wanted that monster cock to fill her, thick, deep, and *now*.

Reaching behind, she grabbed his straining erection and brought it to her sex.

Smooth, broad, hot, the head of his cock spread her, slipping in her wet readiness. She trembled with anticipation.

She could just imagine how glorious all that masculine fire would feel, buried inside her. Her body exploded in desire. "I want you to do this. Do it, now." She circled her hips, pulling him in another inch. "Daniel, I *need* you. *Please*."

With a raw groan, he drove himself into her.

He impaled her to the hilt. Her whole body erupted with pleasure. She broke out in a sweat as heat flushed through her.

He thrust again, a long, hot slide of urgent sensation. She felt every hot inch going in and loved it, moaning with each vein and bump that stretched her.

Then he began to move. His thrusts were powerful, smooth, regular. Assured. He gripped her hips firmly to hold her for his driving rhythm.

"More." She ground herself against him. "Faster."

"Faster? Or *harder?*"

As he always had, Daniel gave her exactly what she needed. "Yes. That."

She rippled in ecstasy, explosions of anguished desire coming faster and closer together, building higher. "*More.*"

"I'll give you more." He drove deep inside her, over and over, primitive and hard. As hard as she could take it, with only a veneer of restraint, as if even his amazing self-discipline had worn thin.

Thin, but not completely gone. He wrapped one arm around her. Dropping a hand to her cleft, his fingers found her hard little bud.

With the last vestiges of his awareness, still thinking—of her.

It rocketed her, screaming, up a mile-high rollercoaster.

To the top.

Hanging there, at the apex of infinity, she could see the vast drop, a climax bigger than the sky itself.

All she had to do was fall.

"Come for me, sweet Zoe," he breathed in her ear, pounding her so hard, their bones seemed to mesh. "Come apart in my arms. I want to see you do it."

She groaned, quivering on the cusp. "You...too..."

"No. I want to watch you come. Come *now.*" His hot mouth latched onto her shoulder.

Like an alpha wolf taking control.

The earth dropped out from under her. She climaxed, *howling*.

Orgasm didn't sing, it bellowed. She shrieked as she plummeted off the edge of the world. A wave of contractions hit her so hard it hurt, each radiating outward with a powerful release. Again, and again, he continued to pump into her, triggering wave after wave until her whole body glowed. Holding off his own orgasm until she was fully satisfied.

The hell with that. She reached behind her, grabbed his hips and pulled.

In her desperation, she yanked so hard she buried him inside her to the hilt. He hit bottom, a sweet, painful tang exploding in her belly, but it worked. He made a strangled sound, music to her ears. She clamped down on her internal muscles, squeezing him as hard as she could.

He roared, gut-deep, and came. Hot, jerking inside her, his eruption extended her own orgasm, rolling it longer, rippling it into infinity.

Her world went white. Noiseless except for a cotton mallet pounding a pillow drum, the thudding of her heart.

The terrible contractions eased. In their place...perfect peace melted through her.

Her heart slowed. She felt mellow, her muscles glowing, her brain clean and new. Sex was always good. But with Daniel it was amazing.

Opening her eyes, she caught sight of herself in the mirror.

She expected the heaving breasts, the flushed skin. Expected the sheen of perspiration and the weary but satisfied expression. Expected the big, happy pupils and thin corona of contented green.

But instead of peridot, her irises were *emerald.*

Her mother's mated color.

The world dropped out from under Zoe a second time. Her limbs trembled.

Mated, without flowers, without candy, without even the whiff of romance.

No. How could this be? She'd done everything right, hadn't she? Anguish stung her eyes. What had she done to deserve this?

Impulsively, she turned to Daniel and burrowed into the safe haven of his arms. He smelled like the best thing ever, like chocolate and flowers and bath oils all in one. Affirming, even if the color of her eyes hadn't already told her, the truth.

Mated.

Without a drop of love. She choked back a sob.

Her worst fear come true.

Chapter Eight

Daniel leaned back against the door and wrapped grateful arms around Zoe, a warm weight against him. He felt wonderful, made new. Happy. Complete. Even in a janitor's closet, that had been much, much more than sex.

With her, it was making love.

"You have the key?"

Her voice came from the depths of his arms, muffled against his chest. He heaved a sigh. Well. The joining of a lifetime to him? Obviously only more sex to her. Maybe not even great sex at that, since he was only human. He released her.

Next time, he'd use his power. Magic would give her an orgasm that would blow her mind.

Idiot. With the threat of the Witches' Council? Witch/shifter sex was taboo, whether he called it lovemaking or not.

There can never be a next time.

Daniel's shoulders slumped mirroring his whole being. His limbs were unaccountably heavy as he picked up his tux jacket and extracted the key.

A stink emerged with it, stinging his nostrils—the acrid stench of evil magic. He suppressed his flinch and opened his third eye.

Ethereal fingerprints glowed blood red on the key.

Damn and blast. Zeus had used *blood magic* to extract the key from Zoe's lovely cleavage. The fingerprints were small, a woman's, meaning the sacrifice was not Zeus' own. Not death, thank goodness, or the bloody color would be tinged with black; but there *was* pain.

With a grimace of distaste, Daniel cleansed the stink off with his mother's scour spell and a whisper of power.

Zoe rubbed her arms, goose bumps rumpling her skin. "Chilly in here."

She'd felt him use his power? Surprise made him pause. Usually, only another witch could detect magic. Maybe their lovemaking had attuned her to him...their *sex,* that was.

"What do you want the key for?"

"Masked ball, remember? Prize going to the most romantic man? Can't unlock the case and award the parchment to the winner without the key."

He winced. The parchment he'd come for, the one he'd now blown any chance to win because he'd behaved like one of her randy high school boyfriends. No, worse. All his sexual expertise, his skills in seduction, learned painstakingly over the years—they'd all vanished simply at the sight of Zoe's upturned hips.

He'd failed her. His heart fell and shame heated his chest as he handed her the key.

"I can't believe, in the middle of all that chest-beating, you thought to pickpocket it. Here I thought you slugged him in a testosterone rage. But instead, you were thinking." She lifted the key to her nose, sniffed it—and then her gaze rose to his and she managed a small smile.

The smile warmed his heart and he started to feel somewhat better.

Her irises were emerald.

Wizards had a saying: "Power shows in the eyes." True for magical beings from witches to familiars to shifters.

Emerald, not peridot. His heart beat faster as he got a strange idea. "What happened to your eyes?"

Her smile disappeared. "Nothing." She turned her head away, shaking it, mahogany tresses rustling against her shoulders. "Sometimes I get emotional. It makes my eyes look darker."

That was true. He knew from his arcane classes that some shifters' eyes were as good as mood rings. An emotional bellwether. But he couldn't help thinking—the most extreme emotion for a wolf shifter was *mating*.

He sucked in a breath, on the edge of something huge...

Then he saw the tear pearling in one emerald eye.

"What's wrong?" he barked. Had he hurt her somehow? It seemed unlikely, given that he was evidently just one more notch on her tail and not a very interesting notch at that.

She sighed and turned from him to pick up her panties. "I'm twenty-nine." She slid the wisp of lace over her long, long legs, over her hips. "My biological clock is ticking extra-loud."

"L-loud?" he croaked. Her panties, gliding up those long legs, reduced his vocal cords to mush.

"Urging me to settle down." She hunted around for her dress. "Find a husband."

Husband. That suddenly sounded like the best title in the world. "That's a bad thing?"

"Well..." She snared her dress and stepped into it. "If my hormones force me to marry, how will I know if I truly love him? If he really loves me? How will I know, years down the road, if it's just sex keeping us together?" She paused pulling the dress up, the knots in her hunched shoulders crying out to him just how important this really was to her.

He instantly needed to help, but he didn't fully understand. Her hormones were urging her to settle down... Did she mean her wolf?

Her wolf will force her to take a mate. Sex and pups, without a choice.

Shocked comprehension coursed through him.

The key was important because it unlocked the parchment.

The parchment was important because it unlocked romance.

Romance was important because *she thought it would unlock the secrets of her heart.*

He ached for her. As he dressed, he couldn't help thinking that Zoe, with all her experience and guts and smarts, didn't understand herself in this one key area.

"On second thought..." She held out the key to him, her vulnerability, her soul in her eyes. "Take it. It'll be safer with you."

He stared at it. It was vital he get the parchment—*the world as we know it will end*. And her handing the key to him was her permission, overriding the geis.

Anyone else, he'd snatch the key. Hell, anyone else, and he'd have used all his talents in seduction, learned from a hundred beauties, to bedazzle her until she gladly gave him the prize.

But this was Zoe—a hurting, *vulnerable* Zoe. And the key she was offering wasn't to a simple prize, but the key to her own heart.

Words clogged his throat. If she'd handed him her physical heart he couldn't have been any more honored—or terrified. He started to reach for it.

He swallowed, hard.

Taking the parchment would hurt her forever. How could he do that to her? His hand wilted back.

The world as we know it will end. How could he *not?*

Which choice is right?

"Daniel, please?" She offered the key again.

She needed his help. Neither choice mattered. He answered as he always had. "Yes, of course." He took the key and tucked it again into his unburned breast pocket.

She exhaled in relief and gave him a small, trembling smile.

"I do understand what this means. You can trust me." He could never abuse her trust.

It nailed a decision that, if he were honest with himself, he'd already made. He needed that parchment, yes. But he'd been hurt badly in high school. He'd never do that to another soul, much less Zoe.

But now how could he get the Quatrain?

* * *

Zoe was surprised how relieved she felt, giving up the key to Daniel—her mate. She turned her back to him in a silent request to zip her dress.

Daniel gave her an efficient zip just as her wolf pulled back its ears and growled.

She jerked. "Something's wrong."

"What?"

"I don't know... Shouting. Coming from the ballroom. Feet running. It's getting louder, nearer. Hear that?" She turned.

He cocked his head, listening. "Now I do." He bent to tie his shoes.

She toed on her own as a voice cut through, high, tight.

"Zoe! *It's gone.*"

Dorine. Zoe hobbled to the door, barely slowing to scoop her heels in with a finger.

Daniel, fully dressed and immaculate, was already opening the door.

The planner ran down the hallway, ducking into each open doorway as she passed. "Zoe, where are you?"

"Here." She waved and trotted toward her.

The moment Dorine caught sight of her, the planner gave a gasp of relief. "Thank goodness. I only turned my back for a moment, I swear."

"What?" Though, from the cold weight in her gut, Zoe knew.

"The parchment."

"Show me." She grabbed Dorine's elbow, surprisingly lean with muscle, and tugged her toward the ballroom. She felt Daniel's comforting presence following behind.

"I don't know what happened. The case is open and I can't find the key."

"You left it in the lock."

"Oh no!" The woman's cheeks reddened, the stink of shame and anger spilling from her. "I'm so sorry—"

"I found out in time and locked the case."

"You did?" Dorine blinked in surprise. "B-but if you have the key, how did the parchment disappear?"

"One of the guests stole it from me." They reached the ballroom, where a crowd buzzed around the front table. As the planner had said, the case was open and empty.

Seeing that void opened an icy hollow in Zoe's chest. Her eyes prickled and her throat thickened. Her prize, gone. She wasn't sure if she meant the parchment, her dreams of romance, or her right to choose her mate.

Or maybe all three.

"I failed," she whispered.

Without the prize, the night was ruined. Her sophisticated, eligible singles would leave. Her shelter friends wouldn't get the romance they'd deserved.

Her step faltered. At the last minute, she turned away. She couldn't bear hearing what they were saying.

"Zoe, it's all right." Daniel clasped her shoulder. "The romance isn't ruined."

Daniel, understanding what was wrong without her saying a word. Trying to fix it, in his own way.

"Thanks for being kind, but—"

"I'm not being kind. Do you trust me? Listen. Really listen."

She didn't want to, but she did trust him. Pricking her ears, snippets of conversation filtered through the haze of her shame.

"I heard the parchment was stolen by a famous cat burglar."

"I heard it was a lost duke, reclaiming his inheritance."

"The Queen of Heart's lover, lost for years at sea."

Daniel bent to murmur in her ear, "It's only added to the mystery and intrigue."

"For now," Dorine muttered ominously. "But what about at midnight? What if the parchment is never found? How will the Queen of Hearts bestow her prize?"

Any hope rising in Zoe's breast died. Dorine was right. Success was a fickle thing.

"Maybe the servers know something," the planner said. "I'll go ask."

Daniel's arms came around Zoe, warming her. "It's okay," he murmured. "We'll find the parchment."

We. Despite already having gotten sex, despite not really needing anything more from her? Startled, she looked up into his face. His star-shot blue eyes were as serious as she'd ever seen.

He'd help her. She needed; he provided.

As he always had.

Her heart gave a painful thump. She hadn't appreciated that in high school. None of her boyfriends had lifted a finger on her behalf. Even her adult men friends were only helpful before sex. Before now, she'd taken Daniel's support for granted–worse, she'd considered it a *turnoff*. Family helped you out, and girlfriends. Who wanted a boy more like family or a girlfriend? That kind of thinking had gotten her the pregnancy scare.

Now she knew better. Dependable and supportive was the sexiest thing a man could be, because with the right man, sex could be lovemaking, and scares could be joyful surprises.

Because the other name for a man who was also family and friend?

Husband.

Desire ignited her veins like a lit fuse. She wanted that, wanted a husband, one who'd make a home with her. A family.

Tethered to Daniel's star-shot gaze, she nodded. She meant more than that they'd find the parchment... *Husband.*

His return smile only held relief. "Good."

He dropped his hands and turned toward the case. He hadn't seen her desire. Preternaturally aware of her needs, this once, he'd been blind.

Unless he'd seen it and was rejecting it. Rejecting *her*.

Like Tommy, damn it.

No. Daniel is different.

Yes. But even if he was, Zoe couldn't marry him. A human, as her mate?

The pack alpha, Scauth, would never accept Daniel. She wiped at suddenly itchy eyes.

Although, if Noah became alpha, he might. Noah might accept them as mates, and...and her wolf might, and Daniel...

He wandered from her to study the open display.

Beast. Her chest froze. Daniel might not.

He returned a moment later, frowning. "The glass isn't smashed. So a key was used to open it. Not your key, because I have that."

She smiled through her unshed tears. Whatever her feelings, whatever *his* feelings, he'd help her, and he'd get the job done. At least she could rely on that. "Zeus?"

"That's my guess."

"But how? You took it back before he could use it."

"He made a copy?"

"Why chase us then?"

"Good question." His lips pursed in thought.

He had insanely kissable lips.

Stupid mated wolf. She shook her head at herself. "And why make a copy if he had the original?"

"Also a good question. Is there only the one key?"

"Yes. The display case is from my motorcycle store, for sunglasses and goggles. I lost the spare months ago and haven't had time to make another."

"Your party planner?"

"I gave her the original."

"Hmm." He strode back to the case and bent to study it closely. Frown deepening, he plucked his handkerchief from his breast pocket, picked a speck of something from the display case, wrapped it in the pocket square and tucked it back in. Always thinking, always observing.

Dork. She smiled, watching his intent face. Wondering how she was going to break the news to him. *I'm mated to you.* She was actually getting used to the idea. She could do a helluva lot worse than the boy who'd cared about her.

Although he'd changed. While the dork part of him was still there, it was covered by a very successful, handsome façade. Athletic and gorgeous, and from the tailored tux and Ferrari, rich, too.

Her smile faded.

Rich, classy, and successful. He could do much better than her now.

Doubt crept in. Sure, he'd always been there for her, was still there for her—but probably only as a friend.

Well. Weren't things were going to get awkward when she started showing up at his home for nightly mated sex?

Awkward? As smart as Daniel is, he'll figure out what's going on. And then...

Would he reject her?

Reject? Her lungs pumped a few panicked breaths.

"You don't look so good." Daniel returned from the case and studied her with the same intense concentration. "Let's sit you down."

She nodded. He took her by the elbow and led her toward the back of the ballroom. She was a strong, independent woman and wolf, but just this once, she leaned on his strength. Besides, her heels were killing her.

They'd almost reached the back exit, and she was anticipating cooler, fresher air, when the door slammed open.

Zeus.

He barged in, panting and disheveled. From the disgusted expression on his cowled face, he'd been dashing up and down Lincoln Memorial looking for them the whole time they were in the closet.

"Run?" she whispered to Daniel, almost glad, almost hoping for another closet and a chance to be together one more time.

One last time.

To her surprise Daniel shook his head with a low growl.

"No."

He let go of her elbow, stalked across the gap, grabbed Zeus—and slammed him bodily into the wall.

Astonished gasps echoed hers. She started to intervene.

Was startled to realize her heart raced and her skin tingled in anticipation, her wolf very near the surface and panting in *delight*.

A crowd of elegant people gathered around her and the two men. Her human, flushed with embarrassment, glanced around. Shockingly, they were more thrilled than appalled, too. Even Ms. Classypants leaned forward, hands clasped in an age-old gesture of excitement.

Zoe didn't know if she was amused or horrified.

Daniel, anger radiating from every taut muscle, didn't seem to care he had an audience. "What you want is gone. Time for you to leave, too. And if I ever catch you sniffing around Lady Mystery again…" He bared his teeth, nailed the cowled man in the eye, and *growled like a wolf.* "You will regret it."

Shock radiated through her flesh. *Daniel has an inner wolf?* From mating with her?

She'd never heard of it happening before.

"I don't know what you're talking about." The barest hint of a submissive whine entered Zeus' tone as he glanced toward the exit, eyes measuring the distance.

Zoe's wolf howled with glee.

"Wrong answer." Daniel grabbed the reeling man, shoved him out the door, and strode out of the ballroom after him. The door slammed shut behind them.

Surprise delayed Zoe a split second before she leaped to follow. She slid through the door silently, shutting it again as Daniel slammed Zeus against the far wall. The hallway was cooler, but heating up fast.

"The parchment is gone. The key is useless to you now, but it always was. You must know that." He leaned into Zeus, using his greater height to his advantage, radiating rage into the cowled man's face. "Tell me everything. *Now.*"

Behind Zoe, the door started to open again. *The crowd seeks to join us.* Her wolf approved—everything important was done in front of the pack, from mating rituals to alpha fights—but Daniel was obviously hanging onto his temper by a hair, and her human didn't want witnesses if things got ugly.

She twisted, caught a man's face in the gap, shoved him back, and pushed the door shut, accessing her wolf's strength to do it. No lock on this side, so she barred the door with her own body.

Zeus surged forward from the wall. "Who the hell do you think you are?"

"A pissed suitor." Daniel planted his fist in the brutal face.

Ripped cowl bounced against the wall, so hard stitching broke and a tuft of dark brown hair sprang out. The man's nose gushed blood. "You fuckin' bastar'. No' again!" One hand, covering his nose, muffled the words.

But in the other, he fisted a wand.

Howling moons, Zeus was a witch.

Witches were bad news. Even a shifter couldn't beat a truly powerful witch. Daniel was in danger. Her stomach dropped out her feet.

But merely human Daniel...

Simply punched Zeus in the nose again.

The witch's wand fell from his hand, hitting the thin carpet with a dull clatter.

For a stunned second, Zeus stood there, eyes wide. Zoe was equally stunned.

Daniel wasn't. He grabbed the witch's raised wrist, twisted to put his hip into Zeus' waist, and neatly flipped the other man to the ground. *Whump*.

Zoe's wolf howled in approval. Even her human body flooded with triumph. Not only had Daniel bested a witch, he'd done so easily. That was *hot*.

"Now talk." Daniel bent, snatched the pocket square from Zeus' breast pocket, and pressed the cloth against his face. "The parchment. The key. Everything."

"Yeh! O'ay." Zeus' chainsaw voice was muffled by the handkerchief. He scrambled back to brace himself against the wall. "Jus' no more hitting." He slurred it, hih-in'.

"No promises. Talk."

Zeus shot him a black look but started talking. "I wanted the parchment." Wah-hed duh par-men. "I tried to magic the thing out of its case. No go. So I light-fingered the key from Lady Boobsalot." He grinned. "Like fondling king-size pillows—"

"One more word like that, and I'll throttle you," Daniel said.

Zeus swallowed hard, grin dropping fast. "The key opened the box, but I couldn't touch the damned thing. Some sorta jinx. So I got a mundane chick to try to take it, but even *she* couldn't touch it."

"It's a geis, asshole," Daniel said. "Nobody magical—or any agent of a magical being—can steal it. Cut to the chase. I don't want to know how you failed. I want to know how you succeeded."

An evil glint sparked in Zeus' eye. "I didn't, *asshole*. You think I have the Quatrain? I don't. Sucker!"

Zoe's heart took a nose dive. Yes, her parchment was missing, and yes, their only suspect didn't have it. But more, there was a magical geis on it—*and Daniel knew it*.

Her hero had a lot of explaining to do.

Chapter Nine

Daniel flashed open his third eye and scanned the brutal-faced man on the etheric. Zeus was telling the truth. Damn and blast. He turned away in disgust.

Only to see Zoe, her gaze narrowed on him.

All the blood drained from his body.

She barred the door he thought he'd locked magically. He had to assume she'd heard everything.

Including bits that could tell a clever wolf a helluva lot about both her parchment and himself.

Time for distraction. "He doesn't have your prize. Let's go." Striding to her, he took her arm and tried to urge her back into the ballroom.

She refused to move, a bad sign.

"What did he mean, he tried to 'magic' the parchment out?"

His stomach froze in his belly. He gave a nonchalant shrug to cover. "Light-finger. Pickpocket. You know, magic fingers."

"I see." Her raised eyebrow, winging above her mask, said she did see, too much.

He grinned, considering the possibility of using sex as a distraction. *Okay, new plan. Don't take her back to the ballroom. Take her to the prep room, throw her onto the couch, and distract the hell out of her*. Something inside him howled with approval.

"What about that name he used? That's the second time he called the parchment the *Quatrain*."

At that, his very blood froze. Thunderation, he was too late.

Her emerald gaze was needle-narrow, searching his face. "Do you know what that is, Daniel? The Quatrain?"

He swallowed hard. He couldn't lie, not to her. He never even considered it, though he knew dozens of convenient, Council-approved misinformations.

But he'd never abuse her trust that way, especially not after what they'd shared in the closet.

Yet what was the alternative? Tell her he'd come to the party because he was like all the rest of the testosterone hulks, not really interested in her, only the prize she offered?

The truth would hurt her. *Unacceptable*.

His brain fought to work through the icy slush of his emotions. It was clamoring, *There's a way*. Dork. Always thinking, even now.

If only he could turn back the clock. Tell her the truth the moment he knew her identity. But he hadn't known she was a shifter, and by the time he had, events were careening out of control.

But since he hadn't told her, he was in a horrible spot, with no good way out. He wanted to bash his own head into the wall, needing a solution that wouldn't hurt the one woman who mattered, but his idiot brain still kept spitting up *tell her the truth*...and the *truth* was, he was just a nice guy to her, a dork, a handy cock for a bit of sex and not particularly good sex at that.

Why would she be hurt if I told her I'd come for the parchment? Because my ego needs her to care that much?

He stopped breathing.

She might be angry, very probably she'd never speak to him again, but she wouldn't be hurt. He'd be hurt, yes. His chest would have a cratering hole, but that was inconsequential.

He gritted his teeth. Didn't matter. Whatever was best for her, he'd live with.

"Walk with me." He took her arm and turned her toward the prep room.

Behind him, Zeus stumbled to his feet and reeled away, maybe looking for first aid. As he didn't have the parchment, he no longer mattered. The curious filtered into the hallway, but they no longer mattered either.

In the prep room, he locked the door, then, to be sure, checked behind the screen. His gaze lighted on the couch, where they'd battled for top. He smiled faintly. Never again, after this. His smile died.

When he was sure there were no physical ears, he checked with his third eye for other bugs, both magical and mechanical. The room was still clean.

He found a couple chairs—he thought for exactly one second about that couch, but if they were to get any talking done, that was out—sat her down and began.

"You know your parchment has visible writing?"

“Yes. Four French words. They mean heart, mind, soul, and key.”

“There’s invisible writing, too. The magical version of disappearing ink.”

“Magical ink...?” She eyed him.

He met her gaze steadily and saw when awareness solidified.

Her eyes widened, those gorgeous emerald eyes, and her hand covered her bosom in an uncharacteristically feminine response. “You’re a witch?”

The sight of her slim, pale hand resting against her beautiful breasts made Daniel want to replace those fingers with his own. Or with his mouth...

But this, first. “Yes.”

She shook her head. “I’d already figured Zeus was, but you...wow.”

“Yeah. Look, I know it’s not likely, but don’t say anything about what happened between us in the closet. To anyone.”

“Why?”

“Do you know about the Witches’ Council?”

She grimaced. “I’ve heard stories.”

“Have you heard about the taboo? Witch, shifter...sex?”

He watched her put it together with what they’d done in the closet, knew what her response would be the moment her hackles went up and she drew an angry breath to speak.

“If you think I’ll let some stupid old Council dictate who I’m with—”

“The punishment is harsh, Zoe. Maximum, death. But there’s a more important matter.”

"*Death?*" The word practically exploded from her. "What can be more important than you and me dying?"

"The *world* dying." He dared take her hands in his, trying to tell her his urgency through touch. "I can't let your parchment fall into the wrong hands. The prophecy it bears is why I originally came tonight, before I knew you were here and your parchment held it."

"Wait, prophecy? What prophecy?"

"When the parchment is treated with the proper spell or potion, it will reveal the Avignon Quatrain, lost prophecy of Jean-Dion d'Avignon."

"A *prophecy?*" She laughed. "Vague, sinister-sounding nonsense."

"Most are. This one, not so much. Avignon's predictions are specific, and they all come true."

Her emerald gaze searched his face, her smile fading. "You believe it. You believe all this. All right, then, if my parchment has this prophecy, why haven't you used magic to get it back? To read it? Come to think, if this Quatrain is so famous, why don't you already know what it says?"

"It was lost for centuries. And I *couldn't* take it. No creature of magic can. There's a geis on it, tying the parchment to its owner—which is you. I also can't read it without a potion or spell. I'll probably need to physically touch it."

She arched a brow at him. "Then how do you know my four-word parchment is your four-line Quatrain?"

"The family seer said so. She also said if the wrong wizard gets his hands on it, it'll be the end of the world as we know it."

She tried a laugh. "What'd I say? Sinister-sounding."

He hated to frighten her, but in this case, not knowing could hurt her worse. "Yes. But also specific."

"Not that specific. What does that *mean*? End of the world *as we know it*. That could be anything from no more earth to people voluntarily giving up their smart phones."

Briefly, he smiled. Faced with a frightening world of power beyond her own, yet she was asking smart, practical questions. "More likely the first, given Avignon. So we have to secure the Quatrain." He searched her eyes, trying to put his own desperation in his gaze. "You must believe it."

Her brows raised. "I don't have to, actually."

His heart dropped. "Zoe, please—"

"But *you* believe it. That's good enough for me."

He blinked, amazed.

"Okay, let's locate that parchment." She stood. "Wait. When you disappeared to figure out Zeus had the key. Did you use magic? Can you do the same thing to find the parchment?"

He was filled with awe. She wasn't panicking, wasn't angry he hadn't told her he was a witch, wasn't fighting him. She was simply listening, accepting. Planning.

Beautiful, practical, and smart. The perfect wife for him. His heart gave a painful thump. If not for the Council's ban.

"I used a find spell, easy enough if you have a good starting point, one with living resonance."

"Like a hair, a fingernail?"

"Yes. In the key's case, the starting point was the napkin, imbued with your living resonance."

She swore. "Which you could use secretly in here. The parchment was in the glass case. You can't do magic there in the ballroom with all those people watching. No convenient nails or hairs dropped?" She snapped her fingers. "What about fingerprints or sweat?"

"Good thinking. But I examined the case. The thief must've used gloves."

"Then what can we do?" Her gaze on him was trusting. She trusted him, trusted his dorky brain to think of a plan.

"Well." He smiled, about to pull the best magic trick of his life, because *she* was his audience. "I did find this bit of trace." He pulled out his handkerchief, carefully unwrapped it to show a single cotton thread.

"From the thief's glove?" She grinned. "Okay, let's find my parchment."

He shook his head. "I need something from you first."

"Something from me?" Her brow furrowed in worry. "What?"

"A promise." His gut dropped with what he was about to ask. She knew he was a wizard now. He'd told her about the Council's taboo on shifter/witch sex.

But what he hadn't told her about was his insane need for her. Since he wasn't sure he could keep his hands off her, he needed her to have restraint for both of them.

Though it would save both their lives, he ached at the thought of never seeing her again.

"This thing between us... It can never happen again."

Chapter Ten

Zoe's heart dropped like a stone. She felt suddenly, unexpectedly exposed, despite her mask. Staring at Daniel, she sank back into her chair. "What do you mean?"

"I'm a wizard, Zoe." His blue gaze, underlined by his dark mask, was stern. "You're a shifter. Coupling between witches and wolves is forbidden. Death-sentence forbidden, as I said before. I think we got away with it last time, but if we do it again we're courting disaster."

"B-but..." Pain stabbed her. "Why did you have sex with me, then?"

His cheeks reddened. Gently, he said, "At first, I didn't know you were a shifter. And then, frankly, I didn't care."

He *wanted* her. Hope ballooned in her chest. "Then can't we—?"

"Not with your life on the line, too. The Council is not lenient on this subject, and the bastards tend to punish the woman more. Unfair, but there it is. I can't risk it."

The rejection sliced her, and she drooped. “No witch has had continuing close contact with a shifter? Ever?”

“Well...”

Just one word, but it was enough. She hung onto that word like a lifeline, her heart beating painfully.

Slowly, he said, “It’s strange, but a man told me a story just tonight. A wizard lived with a shifter and even had a child with her.”

A *child*. With Daniel. At that moment, it sounded like heaven. “Okay. Let’s do it.”

He was already shaking his head no. “She worked for him as a live-in maid. We’d have to pretend to be strangers.”

Ice settled in her stomach. “Oh.” Her voice emerged very small from her tight throat.

“I’m sorry. But it’s for the best.” Daniel rose to his feet, his face more a mask than the one tied over his eyes.

Steeling himself against what had to be done, or did he really not care?

“You won’t be completely safe until I find the parchment. I’m going to cast that locater, now.” He paused, gaze anywhere but her. “You have to go.”

“I do?” The cool, detached tone made her uncomfortable. She rose, too. “Why?”

“Magic sends out a trace on the etheric, like a sonic boom. I don’t want to chance snaring the attention of any nearby witches while you’re here, especially any Council Enforcers.”

“But if we’re not kissing—”

“I don’t want anyone getting even a hint of a wrong idea.”

"Oh." She made her way to the door, cold at the thought this might be one of the last times she'd see him. "I suppose."

Then, as she left the room, he looked *relieved*.

She stopped in the doorway. Chest throbbing painfully, needing his reassurance, she tried to catch his gaze.

Tell me we'll work it out. Whatever it takes. That, like high school, you'll stick until we *get this.*

His back was to her, studying a pan on the table. His mind was already on his magic.

Pain flooded her. He'd axed any fledgling romance between them, and now he'd shut her out of his mind. She was so afraid the next step would be to end the only thing they had left.

Their friendship.

Choking back a sob, she shut the door. A shiver rumpled her flesh just as the door locked with gentle finality.

Ice in her veins, Zoe stared at the locked door. Mating without romance, her worst fear? Right. She laughed without humor, nearly sobbing it.

Mating a man who didn't want her at all was a hundred times worse.

God. Was this what Daniel had felt when she'd brushed him off in high school? Pain throbbed harder with each beat of her heart. Not that she'd ever been as bad as the other girls, but she'd blithely taken his help and hadn't given him much thought beyond that.

Her nose itched with tears, her eyes prickling in her mask. She thumbed the corners of her lids, her thumb coming away wet.

When her boyfriend, Tommy, had dumped her, Daniel had picked up the pieces. Offered, not just marriage, but something more important—respect. Support. Real, committed friendship.

A partnership, a *we* that transcended them both.

Now he'd shut her out.

God. His helping her—didn't matter. His always, *always* being there for her—didn't matter. Romance—*didn't matter.*

More than anything, she wanted their relationship whole again.

She wanted to go back to that united *we*.

Her heart beat a pained pulse. *We.*

We was a two-way street. Him doing things for her, but also *her* doing things for *him*.

"What can I do for Daniel?" she asked out loud.

He'd wanted the Quatrain. His magic would locate the parchment, but she had resources, too.

Specifically, her wolf's nose.

Paper was made from wood pulp, but parchment was prepared animal skin. Even after centuries, it had the distinct odor of leather plus the caustic lime used to prepare it.

All she had to do was track the scent from the case to whoever had it. She hadn't noticed the trail before because she hadn't been fixed on it, blended with the heat and perfumes of human bodies and the food from the buffet tables.

But now she'd do her damnedest to pick it out of all those scents. Wouldn't Daniel be surprised?

Excited, hope renewed, Zoe made a beeline for the ballroom. As she neared the case, she sniffed, accessing her wolf to sort through the odors. The press of bodies was heavy here, the air laden with emotional drama from the theft.

Those odors all but drowned out those of the parchment, and for several overlong moments she turned in place, trying to find a lead, doubting her abilities.

Then she caught the acrid, alkaline edge of lime. She sniffed, drawing it in. The parchment's odor was mixed in with another scent, familiar...

Hell. *Dorine.*

Her wolf howled. The hunt was on.

Chapter Eleven

The elements of Daniel's Locate Object spell were still out, the canned heat and lancet and chafing dish filled with water.

But he needed more than a simple *where* for Zoe's parchment. He needed a *who* and *why*.

Unprepared to meet Zeus, everything had nearly burned in chaos. Daniel wasn't going in blind this time. His locater spell needed more finesse.

Time to call on the expertise of a witch princess who'd been top of her class at Nostradamus U, until she'd given up magic. His cousin, Sophia Blue, was a banker now. He still didn't know why.

He slid his phone from his tux breast pocket and placed the call.

"What is it, Daniel?" Sophia answered, sounding grumpy. She'd been grumpy ever since she'd gone into the mundane sector.

Usually, he tried to jolly her out of it. Now he just said, "Had it ever occurred to you that banking might not have been the best choice for a witch?"

"Has it ever occurred to *you* to get reduction surgery for that nosiness?"

"We're family," he replied. "I have a right to be as annoyingly intrusive as I want. I need your help with a spell."

"Daniel, you know I don't do magic anymore."

"Don't, can't, or won't?"

"Can't," she admitted. "So, while I'd love to help you—"

"Help me form it, then."

A pause. Sounding grudgingly intrigued, she asked, "What kind of spell?"

He almost smiled, even with everything at stake. He'd piqued her interest, reinforcing his notion she should never have given up magic in the first place.

Briefly, he wondered what that *can't* meant. Nothing outside a council Enforcer could strip a witch of her powers, or if Sophia had voluntarily done a complete Evacuate, unheard of for a witch princess.

Daniel shook his head. Fodder for a future conversation. "I need a locater, but not a simple one. I need a where, plus a who and why."

She groaned. "Why not throw in how and when? Daniel, a double Find is hard enough. You want a triple?"

Like map directions, adding another question was like creating another endpoint—plus routes between it and the original points. One question, one route. Two questions, three routes. Three questions, six routes.

"A triple," he said firmly. Then, because it *was* difficult, he stroked her ego a bit. "If anyone can do it, you can."

"Such sweet talk. How can I resist? Does this have to do with the Quatrain? Of course it does," she said, answering her own question. "Have you found it? Is it really Avignon's prediction?"

"Yes. Invisible except for the anchor words on a parchment. There's a geis on it."

"It's cursed?" Sophia whistled. "Let me guess. An injunction against magical theft?"

"Got it in one. Can't be stolen with magic, but also no one with magic can steal it. Wizards, witches, shifters, familiars, or any of their agents...they can't take it without the owner's permission. Yet someone did."

She sucked in a breath. "A mundane? Why are we wasting time talking? Are we using the parchment's starting point itself?"

"No. A representation. A thread."

"Because this wasn't hard enough already. I think I hate you."

"Yeah, there's another complication. The parchment is owned by a shifter."

"Stars and planets, Daniel. You don't ask for much, do you? I'd love to help you, but I put my advanced spell books on consignment."

"C'mon, Sophia. You studied magic like a fiend most of your life. You memorized everything you could get your hands on."

She blew a disgruntled breath. "I used to think it was sweet that you paid attention. Now I think it's a pain in the ass."

"You love the challenge."

"Yeah. Maybe. All right, let me think." Sophia's silence was punctuated by the clomp of her bankers' heels hitting the floor as she paced. Fingers snapped. "Got it. A variation on Knuth's Advanced Find algorithm. 'From this thread and by my blood, find the rose from prophecy's bud, show the who and why as well, for Avignon's truth I bind my spell.'"

"Thanks, Sophia. I owe you."

"No, you don't, Daniel. This is what family does. Help when we're needed. Well, as long as you're not too obnoxious about it." She paused. "Be safe."

As safe as I can, he thought as he ended the call.

The water had been fouled by his search for the key. He'd have to dump it before refilling from the carafe. He left the prep room with the dish, headed for the bathroom, prepared to make excuses to Zoe as he passed her.

She wasn't there.

On the one hand, he was relieved; he could get on with his work. On the other, she'd seemed hurt. Impossible that she'd care for a human dork. Still, he'd have to make it up to her, later.

Except... He paused as reality knifed him.

They had no later.

Angry, he dumped the foul water in the bathroom and wiped the chafing dish with a thick serviette. Unless they tried Jayden's method. It would be complicated. And even if she wanted to risk it, what about any children they might have?

Children. His heart clenched. Miracle of miracles, him a father...and he and Zoe would have to pretend to be strangers.

Pain clutched him. Something deep inside howled against rebuking his own wife, his own children. His inner wolf?

Zoe's life was on the line. Work to do. He shook all his feelings, his doubts, away. For now.

Returning to the prep room, Daniel poured the rest of the carafe's water into the pan and set it over the flame.

Carefully he unfolded his handkerchief, picked out the thread with his fingernails, and dropped it into the water. Stirred the liquid three times.

With the lancet, he pricked his finger. Holding it over the water, he opened his third eye, and recited the incantation as the first drop of blood fell.

* * *

Dorine's scent was much fresher than the parchment. Zoe followed it to the south service entrance—heard running footsteps and looked left, down a long corridor.

The party planner sprinted toward the end, where she threw open a door and dashed outside.

"Dorine!" Zoe sped down the hallway.

She threw open the door and spun into the courtyard just as Dorine reached the door on the other side.

"Damn it, Dorine." Zoe ran after her, stumbling in her high heels. "*Wait.*" She kicked them off as the planner tore open the far door.

The woman glanced over her shoulder. Seeing Zoe, her face paled with guilt. Spinning away, she ducked inside the far wing.

Zoe swore again. Only her wolf could catch Dorine now. Scanning for witnesses and seeing none, she prepared to shift.

Werewolves were human and beast, two halves making one whole like two halves of one brain. To shift, Zoe mentally hunched her human down and let her wolf expand until it enveloped her human, coming "outside."

When the animal manifested, she looked exactly like a natural wolf, although her human brain stayed dominant in the form, just like her wolf's senses continued to function when she manifested as human. From the outside it appeared as if shifters actually moved blood and bone between the two forms, but it was really a magical change. Her human stayed intact, clothes and everything.

Her human body tucked in while her wolf unfurled like a flowering rose. Because she was in the line of alphas, it took her less than a second to transform.

Her wolf bounded across the courtyard in half the time her human could've run it—and a third of the time her human could've run in heels and her rubber band of a dress.

She lost time shifting back to open the far door, and since shifting took energy, she was panting and dragging her tail by the time she hit the upper terrace.

Even so, she'd narrowed the gap. Dorine was just disappearing down the south set of stairs.

Zoe took a step after her—and trod on a canapé some asshole had dropped. She slid, her heart skipping a beat, and nearly turned her ankle.

She tried to scrape the damned thing off as she ran—or rather limped—across the terrace. The stupid creamed goo refused to come off.

Grudgingly, she slowed to a walk, squishing every other step. She got to the top of the stairs in time to see five people come together on the lower terrace.

Three men and one woman ringed Dorine. All four of them were dressed and masked for the ball. One man wore a domino, one had a dark purple nose she recognized as the drunken marquess, and the third...had an off-kilter nose in a ripped leather mask.

Zeus. Zoe bit off a curse of rage.

Dorine held up a scroll case.

The rage tore through. "You damned *traitor*." Zoe dashed for the stairs, skidding awkwardly and barely catching the railing in time. Chafing, she hobbled down the steps. "Auctioning off *my* parchment?"

"My parchment, now." Dorine's gaze followed her, cautious but not afraid, a small smile on her lips.

Zoe was going to wipe that smile off her planner's face—with her claws. "I trusted you. I *paid* you." She stumbled onto the lower terrace and skidded again on her canapéd foot.

"Ms. Blackwood. Stop right there." The planner raised her arm.

It wasn't her cool tone that stopped Zoe dead in her tracks.

It was the gun barrel aimed straight at her face.

* * *

As Daniel's blood hit the water, an image slammed into him, so strong it nearly threw him off his feet.

The lower terrace. Zoe and her party planner. And a gun.

Dorine held a gun on Zoe.

The lancet dropped from his shocked hand, clattering to the floor.

Zoe needs me.

But the spell was incomplete, and the glove thread was already locked in by the first drop of blood.

He needed to finish the spell. He reached for his wand, to draw the fire, water, and blood together. If he didn't finish, it would break, leaving the thread sterile. No second try.

Zoe is suffering.

Without the thread, he might never find the Quatrain...and the *world* would suffer.

But Zoe needs me.

But the world...

Ah, fuck it.

Daniel spun and dashed out of the room. The spell broke. He'd lost his only chance to find the Quatrain, but it didn't matter. Only Zoe mattered.

He flew through the building, to the terrace and across it. Even as he pounded down the stairs toward the lower terrace, his breath rasping and heart hammering, he knew the Quatrain had *never* mattered as much as knowing Zoe was safe and happy.

All those years, painfully erecting a shield over his heart. None of it mattered.

What mattered was doing whatever it took to make sure Zoe was safe and happy.

Whatever it took.

* * *

Zoe held up her palms in surrender.

Or rather, mock-surrender. Shifting healed minor injuries including small gunshots. She eyed Dorine's finger on the trigger and gauged her moment.

"This isn't a 9mm bullet, Ms. Blackwood. My gun fires fifty-caliber ammunition. I'd guess that would put a hole even in you."

Damn. "I guess it would." But Zoe had stalked chancier prey before. Using careful, tiny steps and gliding footwork, she slid closer to the woman without her being aware she was moving. The footwork would've been easier without the smashed cream cheese on her sole, but she managed.

"Zeus I recognize." She talked to distract them from her movement. "And Lord Sash, though I can't believe I actually invited him. But who are the rest of these people?"

"None of your business." Dorine smirked.

"Fair enough. Tell me this, though. Why are you auctioning my parchment? The illuminations are nice, but it's not priceless."

Dorine shrugged. "For some reason, a lot of people are willing to pay a lot of money for it. I like money. And apparently, I'm the only one who could actually liberate the damned thing."

The woman buyer sniffed. "I'd have snatched it weeks ago, but there's a hex on it. My principal's intent prevents me."

The geis. A witch couldn't steal it, and apparently not even a mundane working for a witch. So Dorine was mundane, and not working on anyone's behalf but her own.

Mercenary bitch.

"Well," Zoe began, "I don't know much about hexes, but I hope your principal's intent doesn't also stop you from collecting the parchment after you pay for it. Because it's still *officially* mine. It would be too bad for you if I'm the only one who can really give it away."

"Not an issue," Dorine said. "I took it, I'm the new owner."

"You hope."

"I *am*." Dorine steadied the gun on Zoe and mimed pulling the trigger. "Or I'll make absolutely sure by getting rid of the *previous* owner."

Even knowing the planner was deliberately trying to scare her, to throw her off her game, Zoe's heart leaped into her throat and thudded painfully. She swallowed the taunt she had been about to make and managed a different tack. "One thing bothers me. If you knew you were going to take the parchment, why leave the key in the case's lock? Someone else could have stolen it."

Dorine rolled her eyes. "That's what I wanted you to think. If I hadn't left it in the lock, the theft would've pointed directly at me."

"And Zeus? If there was a hex preventing magical theft, why'd he want the key?"

"The idiot thought I needed it to extract the parchment. He was going to blackmail me, the key for an exclusive bid on the parchment. I told him I believe in the free market." She grinned at Zeus, not nice.

"But you did need the key." Zoe edged nearer. "I locked the case."

"I'm not stupid, am I? I made a copy."

"Smart." She was in striking distance. "So you could've taken the parchment at any time? But you waited until closer to the auction."

"Which is happening now. This girl talk has been fun but enough stalling." Leaving the gun pointed at Zoe, she waved the scroll case at the four people around her. "The bidding has reached two million. Do I hear two-point-two?"

Dorine's attention was only split, but Zoe knew she wasn't going to get a better opportunity. She lunged, putting her wolf's strength into her calves.

She'd forgotten the canapé. She slipped and launched forward instead, her arms flailing.

"Damn it!" Dorine fired.

Zoe twisted midair. The bullet skimmed along one rib, leaving a long, searing flame of pain. She gasped but managed to tuck herself into a roll, planning to hit pavement then spring up to deal with Dorine.

She hit Dorine first. Her momentum knocked the firearm out of the planner's hand, sending it skittering across the terrace.

But it also put her flat on the ground.

The four buyers scattered to the sides of the terrace. Dorine screamed, "You fucking bitch," and kicked her in the ribs.

Zoe rolled away, calling on her wolf to bounce to her feet. Her wolf was already healing the bullet wound.

Dorine pursued her, whapping at her with the scroll case as if she was batting at flies.

Rhythmically. Zoe gauged the timing. Swat. Swat. Swat—*now*. She snatched the scroll case.

Dorine didn't let go. She wrenched back on the case, yanking it from Zoe's grasp but also putting herself off-balance.

The dominoed stranger ran toward them, apparently seeing his opportunity. He tried to grab the case.

Dorine swung it away.

Right into Zoe's face, clocking her.

Shock. Pain ringing. Zoe stumbled back, grabbing the planner's wrist as she fell. They both went down, Zoe pulling Dorine on top of her.

Dorine scrabbled, trying to escape. Zoe, when she realized what she'd done, held on for dear life.

"Girl fight," the sashed-up creep crowed.

"Yeah," Zeus said. "Show those goodies."

Zoe glanced down. Damn her paws. Her neckline had lost round one.

Using her hips, she levered Dorine off. She held onto the planners wrists and flipped them, landing on top so hard it knocked the air out of the smaller woman.

While Dorine tried to suck in a breath. Zoe grabbed for the case. The woman thrashed her arms, making it impossible.

Exasperated, Zoe snared the mercenary's upper arm with both hands and ran her grip up like a sleeve. When she controlled Dorine's wrist, she levered the case away from her.

With a triumphant crow, Zoe sprang to her feet, scroll case in hand.

The marquessy guy hooted. "Wave at me, big girl."

She gave him a cocky grin and waved—until Lord Sash reached out to honk her like a bicycle horn.

"I am not some crappy radio!" She yanked up her bodice with one hand while cocking the fisted scroll case to punch out his lights.

He hopped back, hands covering his nose. "Don't hurt me! Your tit was asking for a honk."

"And your face is begging for my fist." She felt a chill at her bikini line. A quick glance down revealed her exposed lace undies. She'd thought Dorine had picked this dress to distract men—but maybe she'd picked it to distract Zoe.

Which it had done admirably.

She gave up on the garment. It didn't matter now. Getting the parchment to Daniel did. She turned to leave and was distracted by chanting.

She returned her attention to the buyers.

Zeus was chanting, his eyes lit almost as if from within by a red fire. "By this tress, oh so fine."

He held a curl of mahogany hair.

Her hair.

A chill crept over her flesh. She didn't know what he was doing, but she knew it wasn't good.

"By this lock, you're locked as mine... *Give me that scroll case.*"

His command rang in Zoe's head. To her shock, her limbs locked like an automaton. Then, slowly, she turned from the marquess. Haltingly stumbled toward Zeus.

Fighting herself the whole way. Losing.

He reached out to take the case. Tears stung her eyes and she couldn't even blink them away.

Losing? She'd *lost*.

Chapter Twelve

"*Freeze.*" Male, commanding as hell, from above. "Step away from her. *Now.*"

Zoe's heart rose in recognition and gratitude. *Daniel.*

The marquessy guy and the two other buyers stiffened, but Zeus snarled, "You're too fucking late, *Hero.*"

Yanking the scroll case from Zoe's frozen hand, Zeus turned and ran.

Zoe tried to pursue, but her legs were still locked. She tried to shout, "Daniel. Go after him!" Her voice emerged as a whimper. She urged him mentally. *Be the alpha for me. Run after him. Hunt him down.*

But Daniel didn't hear. He drew a black, wire-wrapped wand from his coat—and threw it.

She groaned. That little stick wouldn't do anything.

Except it wasn't a stick sailing through the air toward Zeus, it was a branch. As it flew, the stick grew to the size of a log.

It smashed the cowled wizard in the head, the *clonk* against his skull audible.

He went down, and stayed down.

Pride swelled in her chest. That was what she loved best about her Daniel. Always thinking.

Always saving the day. She should have trusted him. She loved him a little more right then.

Oh God. *I love him.*

He plunged down the stairs toward her. "I saw a gun. Are you all right?"

"I think so." Surprised, she said again, "I'm fine now. Zeus froze me, but the spell must've killed when you dropped him." She tested all her limbs, wiggling them. "Yes, back to normal." Although the shaking nearly popped her breasts out again. She sighed.

Lord Sash grinned. "N-i-i-ce."

"You know what'd be nice?" Daniel stalked to the smaller man and gently brushed along his sash as if cleaning it. The medals tinkled suggestively. "You disappearing, permanently."

The marquessy guy turned his grin on Daniel—abruptly sobering at his needle-thin glare. "Sorry." He raised both palms and backed toward the villa's stairs. "I'll go."

"That way." Daniel pointed down, toward the street.

"Right! That way." He started running and didn't stop until he was out of sight.

Her wolf approved.

At that moment, Dorine edge toward Zeus—and the scroll case lying in his limp hand.

Ripping out a snarl, Zoe launched herself onto the planner.

Eyes widening, Dorine spun mid-run and took off after Lord Sash.

The two remaining buyers melted away into the night.

Zoe landed in a crouch. "I'll get them." She prepared to spring.

"No need," Daniel said soothingly.

"But they'll get away!"

"Just for the moment. I'll send these to the Witches' Council." Daniel opened his fist to reveal four hairs.

Zoe rose, gazing at his palm in awe. "How'd you do that?"

"Pickpocket spell. Although I collected two personally. The Marquess's, and..." He leaned down to pluck a single hair from beneath Zeus's cowl. Even unconscious, Zeus winced.

Zoe retrieved the scroll case from Zeus' limp hand. She revealed Daniel's wand laying next to the man's head, normal size now. She scooped it up and handed it to him. "That wand thing was a pretty slick trick. Why didn't you simply blast him?"

"Security cameras." He flicked a glance at the mounted electronic eyes. "They cover the terraces, but not the air above them." He nodded at the case. "The parchment is in there?"

She peeked inside. "Yes. *My* parchment." It was hers to give away again. She could finally get the romance she'd desired with her whole heart. "You still want it?"

He frowned. "Yes."

She reminded herself romance was a two-way street.

And sometimes, that could be fun. She grinned and waved it in front of him. "Then you'll have to earn it." She turned and bounded up the stairs.

Hoping he followed.

She ran all the way to the prep room, buoyed by a reckless excitement.

A lot like the night she'd told her boyfriend she thought she was pregnant and got dumped. No reason to believe this would turn out differently.

Except this was Daniel.

His strong breath and steady footfalls behind her gave her hope. She ran lightly, dreaming what she'd say. What he'd say.

Your patient devotion, Daniel, all those years ago. Your absolute support. I know how great a gift that was, now. I wasn't mature enough to appreciate your love in high school. Now I am.

Zoe, he'd say. *I still love you.*

He followed her into the prep room.

Where he shut the door with a decidedly upset slam.

She spun, suddenly unsure. His back was to her.

"What did you mean, Zoe?" His words were neutral, but his back was stiff, and his tone was angry. He locked the door. "What did you mean, *earn* the parchment?"

"I-I..." Her own imagined sweet confession faltered on her tongue.

"What do you want from me? Flowers, candy, sweet words of love?" He turned then. The fire in his eyes was part arousal, part fury. "I'm not that boy any more, Zoe."

Her heart beat a pained thump. "I know." Her shoulders seemed to fold in on her. Her declaration of love seemed naïve, now. Maybe even pointless.

He grimaced. "Whatever you plan to do with that parchment tonight, I have a job to do first. I need to see the prophecy on it."

The prophecy. He'd stay with her until it was revealed. Okay, she still had time. Time to try to reconnect with him. Convince him to give *them* a chance.

She offered him the scroll case. "Are we safe to be together here? From the Council?"

"No. But as you so clearly pointed out, that's yours. If I want to read the prophecy, I do it in your presence. Putting *your life...*" His jaw worked. "Putting both our lives in danger. Unless you're turning it over to me." He barked it like a challenge.

She swallowed hard. "No."

"Then I'll do the best I can. I'll sweep for psychic eyes and physical bugs, and we'll have to hope like hell there are no Enforcers physically nearby."

Closing his eyes, he turned in place, making tiny gestures, finally flicking fingers toward the ceiling then the floor. The task seemed to calm him.

Admiration filled her, watching her mate work. He was careful, thorough, yet efficient.

A moment later he opened his eyes. "All right. Put the parchment over there on the table. I need to call for some specialized help." He got out his phone.

"You're going to reveal the writing here? Now?"

"Before this, I expected to take the parchment home and work on it at my leisure. Now, you've left me no choice. If I can't have the parchment, I'll at least know the prophecy. Find out how bad it is."

Her hopes fell. Once he knew the prophecy, nothing would keep him here. She had to make her case now. But what would she say? *Daniel, I need you.* That would work, but it was no longer how she wanted to define their relationship. *Daniel,* we *need you.*

He used his thumb to activate the phone. "Sophia? I need another spell."

Zoe waited while he set up his equipment, pouring fresh water into a chafing dish. Standing there with the gnawing fear in her that her mate might walk out on her, she clutched the case. Her parchment, in her family for generations, contained a prophecy by a wizard even she'd heard of. She couldn't help but wonder what it would say, but she dreaded the moment it was revealed.

Cudgeling her brain for a way to keep him with her, she slowly extracted the parchment and flattened it on the table.

A few *um-hms* later, Daniel ended the call and turned to her.

"This takes a drop of blood, not only from me, but from the owner of the parchment. You. Do you mind?" He produced a lancet from his pocket.

Wordlessly, she offered her finger. He poked quickly and efficiently, the stab so slight she hardly felt it.

Yet the act felt oddly intimate.

Rich red blood welled from her fingertip. Gathered. Fell.

She tried again to talk about *them*. "Daniel, about high school..."

The drop hit the water with a sparkle that dazzled.

"High school is over, Zoe." He repeated the action with his own finger.

At his words, her spirits plummeted.

His blood fell beside hers, also sparkling. But as he extracted his wand, something strange happened.

The two lobes of blood merged, like a tiny heart.

Zoe's own heart contracted painfully. If she'd given high-school Daniel a chance with her, would he have drawn a heart like that, maybe even with a ZB+DL?

He was no longer that dorky boy—that adoring boy. Her heart gave another lurch, for what might have been.

Had she but known to cherish it.

"What...?" Daniel's star-shot blue gaze zeroed in on the heart. He leaned closer, his lips parted slightly.

Was he as moved by that small symbol as she? Her hope lit briefly.

Then his mouth tightened, and he straightened, poked the wand into the water, and stirred until the blood was dissolved.

She ached for that tiny destroyed heart. For her broken hopes.

He lifted the wand from the water. Positioning the stick above the first word on the parchment, COEUR, he tapped its tip on it. The letters shimmered, changing to the English HEART. A bit of water was left behind, beaded on the word.

He returned the wand to the water three times, tapping each keyword. ESPRIT became MIND. ÂME changed to SOUL. CLÉ became KEY.

Once more he dipped the wand in the water. Tapping the word HEART three times, he said, "Show me heart."

Writing appeared, wavering at first, then solidifying into a flowing masculine script.

Zoe blinked. "HEART beats for a wolf and a Blue."

"Hmm. Suggestive, isn't it?"

"Wolf, like me? But you're no Blue."

"No. But my cousin is. Let's see what the rest has to say."

He repeated the procedure for the other three lines until the complete prophecy was revealed.

HEART beats for a wolf and a Blue
MIND is focused by Light
SOUL belongs to those who are True
The KEY unlocks the Night.

"What does that mean?" Zoe tilted her head, as if that would show her the words in a new light. She glanced at Daniel.

His face paled. "Night...usually means magic."

"A key to magic? I thought you said the world would end as we know it."

"This is far worse." His voice rasped.

"What do you mean?" She was startled by his serious tone. "Isn't this just a spell to make a magical key?"

"More likely a list of talisman components."

"Pieces?" She frowned at him. "Put together, they make some sort of a key to magic?"

"Not just *a* key. *The* key." His gaze came to hers.

The worry she saw there deepened her own anxiety. "What does that mean?"

"The best we can hope for? The key gives its possessor unlimited magical power."

"Unlimited power...? But what if a witch like Zeus gets his hands on it?" Being completely at his mercy was chilling enough. She imagined the brutal-faced man able to do anything, absolutely anything he wanted.

She felt sick at the thought. No one would be safe.

"We'd still have a chance. To fight him, to steal it away from him. But there's another interpretation."

"Worse than that?"

"The key unlocks magic—in other words, reveals it."

"To mundanes?" Even she knew that was bad. "Wouldn't that be the end of magic?"

"Yes. No more spells, no more familiars, no more shifters. No more magical beings at all."

"I'd lose my wolf?" Her throat thickened. She swallowed past it. "You'd lose your magic?"

"If we're lucky." His grim expression scared her more than his words. "We're magical beings, Zoe. No more magic? Maybe no more *us*."

Adrenaline goosed her at that. "Don't you know?"

He shrugged with a twisted smile. "That's one of the annoying things about a prophecy. Only time will tell the full story."

Biting her cheek, she stared at the first line again. "Are you sure Heart couldn't be about us? I'm a wolf, and your eyes are a gorgeous star-shot blue."

He slanted her an exasperated look. "Cataclysmic prophecy, and you're noticing that *now*?"

Embarrassment heated her face. She covered it with a question. "Then who's the wolf?"

"I won't know until the prophecy fulfills. But one thing is clear enough. There are people, powerful, possibly evil people, who are also after the prophecy." Even his twisted smile disappeared, replaced by a grim line. "I'll need to solve the riddle first, to keep the key safe."

A shiver of dread rolled over her. Followed by alarm at his change in words—*I'll* need to solve the riddle, not *we*.

"Daniel? I know you got what you came for..." She rolled up the parchment, not quite brave enough to look at him. "Are you leaving it with me?"

He was silent as she returned the scroll to its case. Silent as she set it case aside. He was silent so long she had to look.

His gaze was on her, that intelligent, penetrating stare, and the grimace was back. "It's yours. The geis is still on it. I couldn't take it from you even if I wanted to." He sighed. "But more, I wouldn't."

She nodded, acknowledging he was as honorable a man as he'd been a boy. "Then I can use it for its original purpose? As a prize for tonight?"

He looked away. "Yes."

Wrong move. Her heart beat harder. She didn't want him to go, but she was losing him. She didn't know what to do.

Uncertainty turned her stomach into a raw pit. She bit her lip. Swallowed hard. All the things she wanted from him. *I want you to romance me. I want you to stay with me.*

I need you to love me.

Maybe she shouldn't try to explain. Maybe she should just go with what worked. "Daniel, I need your help. I need you to..."

Her words dribbled off because, still not looking at her, he busied himself cleaning up the spell-casting equipment.

It wasn't working. Even the tried and true had failed her, and she was left floundering.

Once he cleaned up, he'd leave. She ached at the thought of never seeing him again.

Why was love so damned complicated?

Finishing, on the cusp of leaving, he lifted his head and his gaze nailed hers. "What is it, Zoe? What do you want me to do this time?" He made it an angry challenge.

Pain hit her. "I'm sorry." Tears burned her eyes. "I don't want you to do anything, Daniel. I just...I just want *you*." She hiccupped a sob.

His lips parted, a dazed look hitting his blue gaze. "Say that again?"

She blinked wet eyes. He blurred in her sight, but at least he was still here. Still talking with her.

She dared touch fingertips to his broad chest, as if she could tether him there with her touch. Searching his face, she tried to figure out what to say to appeal to him. She couldn't read his unfathomable star-shot gaze. Heaving a watery sigh, she gave up, and simply made her appeal.

"When we were younger, I wanted things from you. I never put my wants into words because I never had to—you gave me what I needed without asking, sometimes before I knew I needed it. All I had to do was say 'I want you to...' and you'd fill in the rest.

Now, for the first time, I'm faced with having to *say* what I need. And I realized something important." Her misery bubbled up into a remorseful laugh. "All these years—I've been starting that sentence all wrong. I don't want you 'to' anything. It's simple. I want you."

"You want me," he echoed on a whisper.

"Daniel...I know we can't be together because of the Council. But before you go...will you give me one last time with you, to remember us by?"

"Us?" He smiled sad, poignant. "Yes." He lifted her off her feet. Carrying her to the fainting couch behind the screen, he laid her on her back.

She had no doubt who would be on top this time.

His palms landed on her thighs. A gentle push parted her legs. He bent his head to her mound.

The heat of his breath scorched her panties. Her sex contracted in anticipation, tingling through her thighs and hips.

He licked her. Her whole body tightened in response, wringing a mewl from her throat. He licked again. Then he licked over and over until she was on *fire,* the panties damp and molded to her. Urgency pooled heavy and hot in her pelvis. Muscles melting, she let her head fall back, too heavy for her limp neck.

The moment she yielded, he slid the skimpy lace from her hips, down her legs, and off. Taking her naked hips, he lifted her to him.

Gave her a deep, open-mouthed kiss.

She moaned, fireworks going off inside. Tonguing her, kissing her, sucking her until she screamed, he loved her with his single-minded intensity until her blood boiled. Until her whole body shrieked with urgency, tensed for release.

"Daniel, I'm ready." She reached down for him, to pull him into her embrace.

He stayed stubbornly where he was, loving her with his mouth. He winched her tighter and tighter and tighter yet, until she *burned* for relief. Writhing in anguish, she gave up and grabbed his head, rubbing then grinding against him, practically riding him.

"Now you're ready." He thrust a finger inside her.

She exploded, short but desperately hot.

While her brain was spinning, Daniel stood. Waving a hand from his crown to his toes, his clothes...disappeared. A moment later, a pile of garments reappeared, neatly folded on a nearby table.

Leaving him clad in nothing but his mask and straining desire. His gaze locked with hers, his starburst eyes so hot they were supernovas.

Howling moon, he's gorgeous. She stopped panting to swallow, hard, and managed, "Can you do that to me, too?"

"No." He knelt between her wet thighs. "Well, I *can*, but I'm not going to. I'm doing this the old fashioned way."

A single hard tug brought down her bodice, exposing both breasts, plump and tight and eager to meet him. He kissed one, then the other, so fast and hungry she burst out in a delighted laugh.

He got down to suckling and she dissolved into a long, low moan as her desire reignited. Snaring fingers through his hair, she pulled him closer, needing more. He answered her unspoken desires as he always had, raking teeth on the edge of her nipple. She yowled.

He raised his head despite her strength. "Did I hurt—"

"*No*. More. Again."

He gave her more, again. Harder. As she lay back, he followed her down, still suckling, until he covered her with his bare lithe body. She petted his hair, releasing a clean masculine scent. She ran her palms over the corded muscles in his neck down to the broad strength of his shoulders, delighting in the contradictory sensations of warm velvet skin over rock hard muscle.

"More," she whispered, bent to his ear. "*Everything*." She nudged his hip with one foot.

He raised himself to hands and knees over her, positioned between her legs. "You're ready?"

The muscular tension in his chest and arms, the straining cock, and most of all yearning in his eyes undid her.

"Oh, yeah."

She wrapped her arms around his neck and her ankles around his waist and *pulled*. He sank into her. She groaned in pleasure, twisting her hips to take him deeper. His thick erection felt like heaven.

Her tugging buried him inside her to his root. He shouted, his voice twining with her pleasured moans.

Pressing her back into the couch, he began riding her in long, undulating waves, lush swipes that ended with a grind of his hips. She panted, her arousal flushing hot blood through her, her skin beginning to dew. His mouth found hers and he kissed her with deep thrusts of both tongue and cock.

She began driving her hips upward in the same rhythm, doubling the friction. He sped up the tempo, and she met him thrust for thrust.

Her body caught fire. Faster and faster, she winched toward the top, her fingers digging into his back muscles, her tongue driving into his mouth, dueling with his so eagerly it caused sparks. She built, and built more, until she couldn't stand it.

"Daniel," she wailed. "*More.*"

He answered her need as he ever had—and yet, as he never had before.

"Oh, I'll give you more." He held his finger before her eyes, the tip haloed with energy.

Magic.

Reaching between them, he touched her sex. Magical power sang straight into her primed body.

Climax took her like a lightning strike. She shrieked as screaming pleasure exploded in her brain, a cascade of starbursts lighting her whole body. Like a fireworks finale, climax boomed on and on until she was exhausted.

As the contractions ebbed into aftershocks, her breathing slowed, and her heated body cooled.

She felt light, happy.

Then Daniel collapsed on her.

"*Oof.* I almost wish for the ninety-eight pound weakling back. Just kidding." She was still happy, but he was a heavy man.

"Mmm." He shifted slightly so that not all his weight was on her. She still felt the thump-thump of his heart as it slowed. It was nice. Comforting. She could see doing this far, far into the future.

With pups playing in the yard, then grandpups. When they were old and their muzzles were gray.

At the thought, she drooped. The sad truth was, they only had tonight.

* * *

Daniel lay beside Zoe, gazing at her beautiful masked face as his heart slowed. He caressed a strand of hair back from her forehead. He'd waited for this all his life, even as he'd argued with himself through the years that one female couldn't possibly be worth it.

She wasn't worth it—she was *more* than worth it.

He'd wanted her to fall in love with him, to want him the way he wanted her. And at last she'd asked, not for him to do something for her, but just to be with her.

She'd finally admitted she wanted him. It made him hope. Hope that she might come to love him. More, she might love him as he loved her. Completely. Forever.

You mean never. *It's forbidden by the Witches' Council.*

His stomach twisted at the thought. With a sigh, he sat up. Even if they loved each other fully, unreservedly, they couldn't be together. For himself, he'd risk it. But not with her life on the line.

She sat up, too, her head down, her hair tousled around her face so that he couldn't see her expression, but her body was slumped.

Relaxed...or disappointed?

Probably disappointed. His spirits plummeted even further. The one thing she'd wanted tonight, that she'd planned for and paid extravagant amounts of money to get—romance. Yet here he was, jumping straight to sex yet again.

But he couldn't stop touching her. Couldn't stop kissing her. *Couldn't stop burying myself inside her, over and over...*

"Zoe..." He sighed. "I'm so very sorry."

"Why?"

"Chivalry isn't dead. Romance isn't dead. I know there's a romantic hero for you out there. And I tried... but with you I *can't* be romantic. I wanted to do flowers and candlelight, but I shot straight to naked and sweating."

She didn't answer him, head still down, face veiled by glossy mahogany hair, more camouflage than her actual mask.

"I'm sorry to lose my chance at the parchment." He took her hands. "But what I'm really sorry about is that I've lost my chance to make you happy."

She still didn't answer. Was she crying? He was, inside.

He released her hands. "I hope Mr. Romance can give you what I can't."

She finally raised her head. Her cheeks were wet. "Daniel. You're still a dork, you know that?"

"Yes." His heart broke. He'd hurt her, without meaning to.

She sighed. "Come on. I have to get back to my guests and reward my best suitor with this parchment."

His chest contracted in pain, this time for himself. Suddenly he couldn't face seeing her present the parchment to someone else. Seeing another man had won her approval. Not that he cared who she gave the thing to, but after that amazing climax, after connecting with her here so intimately...well. Seeing her eyes light up gazing at another man felt like a particularly cruel sort of agony. "I'll leave you to it, then."

"No! No, don't go yet. Th-there might still be a witch out there who wants to get her hands on this. Wait until I've handed it off?"

"Well...yes, of course. You need me?" Covering his dismay, he stood, waved his hand, and was immediately dressed.

"I do." She smiled, but it was sad. Standing, her dress fell to her waist. She glanced over her shoulder. "With all my squirming, the zipper came undone. All that talk about not wanting you to do anything, and now I have to spoil it. Could you...?" Holding up the bodice, she turned her back to him.

He zipped the dress, covering her creamy skin, then tugged her skirt straight. It was hard not to run his hands over her, push her back onto that couch, and take her again.

If they moved in together, they could do that every day of their lives.

But no. Even if she somehow miraculously fell in love with him, the only way they could be safe was if she played his servant. He'd never live like that.

She found her panties, skimmed them on, then went to retrieve the scroll case. "Let's go."

Unlocking the door, he let her out. She swiveled past him on her long, long legs, his hopes leaving with her.

He followed. Even though he should be pursuing the first piece of the prophecy. Even though seeing her gaze into another man's eyes with love would shred his heart.

She needed him, and so he followed.

Chapter Thirteen

Outside the ballroom door, Zoe turned to him.

"Daniel, you said you wanted to give me romance. For once, you got it wrong."

That hit him like a blow. "I'm sorry."

"Don't be. It's not your fault, it's mine. I *said* I wanted romance. I *thought* I wanted romance." She gave a sad little laugh. "I was lying to myself."

"What?" His emotions were a confused jumble.

"I should have seen it sooner. My words and actions didn't line up. I kept saying I wanted romance, but instead of doing it, instead of seeking out dashing men with flowery words, I kept running away to have sex with you."

His heart paused. He whispered, "Should have seen what?"

"The truth. What I *truly* wanted was a *connection*. Wolves mate regardless of love. I was worried that without romance, I wouldn't know what a real connection was. But I do." She brought his hand to her chest. "You showed me, Daniel. You've always shown me."

And now that she'd recognized it, she could move on. His heart beat in renewed agony. "I understand."

Now she could mate with a wolf. He panted past the pain.

"When you zipped me up, you were acting like a brother or lady's maid. But I know you're not either of those. Daniel, even if I acted as your maid, you'd still know I was your mate."

"M-mate?" His breath stopped.

She nudged him. "Could be fun role play."

Her eyes. Once the green of new grass and the hope of spring...now emerald, and they'd stayed emerald too long to be fleeting emotion.

That wasn't simply sex they'd had, not even in the closet.

They were mated. Married, in the customs of her people. For life. His heart thumped an erratic beat, on the edge of forever.

And in the custom of *his* people?

He took a deep, painful breath. His heart slammed into a staccato tempo. The Witches' Council would be sharpening all their axes.

Mated. Forever.

"Wolves and wizards can't be together," he began. "It's a death penalty..."

His voice died, the importance of his answer so overwhelming to him, he almost couldn't put it into words.

"Oh. Of course." Her voice was so small and hurt. She dashed the few steps to the door and threw it open to the ballroom.

The lofting refrain of "Some Enchanted Evening" filled the air.

She stopped just inside, staring at the couples dancing.

Daniel strode into the ballroom after her. Taking her shoulders, he turned her toward him. "You didn't let me finish."

Her eyes came to his, confusion clouding them.

"We can't be together, but the hell with that." He went down on one knee before her. "Lady Mystery, I love you."

Around them, the swirling couples slowed. Came closer. Conversations fell off, as if everyone wanted to hear what he had to say.

He raised his gaze to Zoe's, loving the deep emerald of her irises, jewels set in her black mask, glittering in the golden light. "I've loved you forever. I never felt good enough for you, and I still don't. But if you say yes, I promise to spend the rest of my life working to help you be happy and fulfilled."

"Yes to what?" she breathed.

"To words I mean with every beat of my heart. Will you marry me?"

Radiant joy in her eyes, she smiled. His heart leaped.

Then she glanced at the attentive faces around them, and her smile died.

His chest hollowed.

In an undertone she said, "We have witnesses. What if this gets to the you-know-what Council? We can't get away with pretending not to know each other."

He wanted to howl. "I don't care."

"*I* do. I don't want to be a wife and a widow in one day."

She was going to turn him down, *again*. His heart shriveled.

He stood. They couldn't live together. Couldn't marry, officially.

Officially. The Council was potent, but it was an official organization, not an omnipotent god.

If the Council couldn't find them, it couldn't punish them.

He chewed it over. Would it work? He'd never consciously put Zoe in danger.

Sophia used to work for the Council. If he and Zoe went on the run, surely she'd know enough to help them stay one step ahead.

On the run. No more living in high style, no more New York lofts or Ferraris.

He'd only be giving up...everything. All those years, fighting for status and acceptance among the cool kids. Gone.

"Daniel?" She cocked her head in question at him, her mahogany hair rippling to one side.

No, not *everything*. He'd have Zoe.

Completely worth it.

He took both her hands and tried to tell her how much she meant to him. "I love you, Lady Mystery. If I tell you I have a way to be together, will you make me a happy man? Will you marry me?"

The orchestra stopped playing. The room was hushed.

The sound of the clock, winding up to strike, dropped into the silence. Her gaze shifted away. "Look at the time."

She turned from him as the clock struck midnight.

His hands fell from hers, dead weights.

And in his chest, his heart turned to ashes.

* * *

Pulse hammering in her ears, Zoe raised her voice to address the assembly. Time to make official what she'd already acknowledged in her heart.

"Good evening, everyone. I am the Queen of Hearts and this is my ball. Tonight, I award this parchment." She held up the scroll case. "I award it to the man who has romanced me the best. A man who romanced me, not with flowers and sweet nothings, but with his constant support, guidance, and commitment. With the light of his love."

Give this to the Light, Zoe. Now the cryptic words that had appeared on the parchment made sense. Daniel Light, but more, the light of her life. Tears welled hot in her eyes.

"I present the prize to My Hero." She turned and handed Daniel the scroll to a smattering of polite applause.

He frowned at it in his hands as if he couldn't understand what it was. What it meant.

"I learned something tonight. This parchment was my idea of a romantic gesture. I thought romance was the single truly beautiful gift between a man and a woman. But you know what? Romance isn't the gift—it's the bow. The decoration for the real gift. A true and constant heart."

His gaze rose to hers. A sheen covered his beautiful blue eyes.

"You've given me that as long as I've known you. Your pure, true, constant love." She took his face in her hands. "My Hero—you asked me to marry you. Do you want to hear my answer?"

His lips parted to speak, but no words came out. He swallowed several times but finally only nodded his bright blond head.

Not asking with words. But he'd given her what she needed for years, without her ever asking. Now, at last, she'd be able to return the favor.

"With this crowd as my witnesses, I present the true prize—my heart. I love you, My Hero. Yes. My answer is *yes*."

Stars of pure happiness burst in his blue eyes. She drew him to her and kissed him before the gathered throng.

This time wild applause broke out. Her heart shouted joyously with it.

* * *

Weeks later, Daniel lay with a sleeping Zoe nestled beside him on the cheap mattress of an inexpensive anonymous flophouse. He was sleepily contemplating how much his life had changed when his burner cell buzzed on the plywood nightstand beside him. He reached for it.

Sophia, along with help from others in their extended family, had discovered Dorine's buyers included the agent of an exiled witch. The buyers were tracked down and interrogated. They didn't give up their principals but there was a hint some of them were very highly placed. That gave Daniel some sleepless nights.

But Daniel and Zoe managed to keep one step ahead of the Witches' Council.

He lifted the cell phone. One text. From Sophia, though the number was unfamiliar.

"GO."

His adrenaline spiked. He woke Zoe and they threw their go-bags into the latest of a long line of second-hand beaters, paid for with cash.

Life on the run wasn't easy. Zoe'd had to sell her business. Luckily, the money from that plus the cash they'd gotten from offloading all Daniel's expensive toys gave them time to figure out a plan. For now, they continued to send money anonymously to her mother. Continued to buy beaters and rent flops.

Continued to live, and love, together.

As Daniel cranked the ignition, a bright flash went off behind them. His delayed-action scrubbing spell, muddying all traces of his and Zoe's presence. When the Council Enforcer arrived, all he'd find was the magical equivalent of dust.

As he drove away, he reached for Zoe's hand at the same moment she reached for his. Their fingers met. Joy surged through him at the connection.

Halloween had brought him some of the worst luck ever, destroying his old life.

But in its wreckage rose a new life.

A hard life, yes, living on the run.

But also incredibly freeing. Stripped to life's bare essentials, Daniel now knew what was truly important to him. Not his Ferrari or his charm or even his magic. Despite the chilling prophecy that cast a pall over them all, he was happy.

Happiest, simply being with his mate. Knowing he loved her. He tossed a quick grin at her, his joy doubled when she returned it with a big smile of her own.

Knowing she loved him in return? The best magic of all.

Dear Reader,
Thanks for reading! My greatest joy as an author comes from you joining me here in my book world. I hope you've found entertainment and pleasure in these pages for a time, and that you'll come back and join me soon.
~Mary

Want to hear about new releases? Sign up for my newsletter!
http://www.maryhughesbooks.com/Newsletter.html

A Request

If you enjoyed this book, I'd really appreciate it if you'd take a moment to review it online. You can help prospective readers find new books to love by writing a few sentences about what you enjoyed.

Thanks for taking the time to do a review!

Curious to find out what happens with the prophecy? Continue reading for the first chapter from *Heart Mates* (Pull of the Moon Book 2) and *Mind Mates* (Pull of the Moon Book 4).

About the Author

Mary Hughes (written Hug-he's but possibly pronounced throat warbler mangrove) writes smart and sassy stories of action and love.

She's a bona fide computer geek and performing flutist. (And piccolo, but we don't talk about that.) When this USA Today Bestselling Author isn't busy finding the missing </> tag or blowing her lungs out, she's on the couch reading or binging on The Flash, Elementary, NCIS, or Wynonna Earp...and petting the cats that inevitably end up on her lap.

Mary's online and would love to hear from you!
Newsletter http://www.maryhughesbooks.com/Newsletter.html
Facebook http://www.facebook.com/MaryHughesAuthor
Twitter http://www.twitter.com/MaryHughesBooks
Instagram https://www.instagram.com/maryhughesbooks
BookBub https://www.bookbub.com/authors/mary-hughes
Goodreads
http://www.goodreads.com/author/show/279140.Mary_Hughes
Website http://www.maryhughesbooks.com/
Blog http://maryhughesbooks.blogspot.com/

Turn the page for a special preview of
Mary Hughes's next Pull of the Moon novel

Heart Mates

Available now from 7th Octave Publishing

To survive, they'll have to find the missing pieces—starting with their own.

Heart Mates

Pull of the Moon, Book 2

Sophia Blue wishes the cute little doggie she's found in her aunt's abandoned magic shop could talk. Maybe he'd tell her if the old woman has wandered off on a walkabout, or if there's foul magic afoot. Odd how the scruffy little fur ball seems to understand Sophia's every word.

Just a few years ago, she might have cast a spell to translate the dog's ear-piercing yaps. But her magic is out of her reach, locked away in penance for mistakenly helping an evil wizard.

Noah Blackwood was the last person to see Sophia's aunt before she hit him with a spell gone sideways. By night he's two-hundred pounds of authority, a respected local pack leader. By day? He's twelve pounds of poof dog. A tasty morsel for the five anti-alpha wolves gunning for him.

The instant the sun goes down and Sophia's eyes meet Noah's, fire ignites between them in an incendiary kiss. But when the evil wizard reappears intent on murder, Sophia must break through killing layers of pain to find her magic. And Noah must reclaim all that he is—even defy the law—to claim the woman his heart knows is his mate.

Warning: Contains a sassy ex-witch princess who hasn't picked up a wand in four years, and a rare alpha wolf who proves attitude knows no boundaries. A little drooling, a lot of panting, and a few nips in all the right places. Flea collar not included.

Enjoy the following chapter from *Heart Mates*:

Noah Blackwood opened the door to the Uncommon Night Owl Bookstore, knowing full well he was walking into trouble.

He'd only been alpha a few days, but already he had a sense for when members of his pack were in trouble—and when they were *causing* trouble. Sure enough, as he glided soundlessly across the threshold of the bookshop, his foot struck broken glass. He scanned the store with a narrowed gaze.

Seventeen-year-old Marlowe stood to his left, beside a front display case. His dirty fingers were wrapped tightly around something, caught in the act of stealing it.

Marlowe was a bully in training and a young man with too much time on his hands.

By bloody tooth and claw, Noah would give the pup something better to do.

As he closed the door and strode toward Marlowe, Noah realized the pack youth was frozen in place, fingers squeezing the thing as if he *couldn't* let go.

And that the thing was a foot-long psychedelic capped tower that looked uncomfortably like an erect penis.

Noah scowled. He wasn't sure what was more unnatural, that frozen boy or the flower-power dildo.

A rattle of beads from the back of the store caught his attention.

"*Mr.* Blackwood." The store's proprietor—Linda Blue, styled herself as some sort of seer—swept apart a back curtain of beads and trundled out. "You'll need to keep better control of your people. You're better than Scauth, of course, but...oh my." As she neared, her hand fluttered to her ample bosom.

Magic flared in his sight, nearly blinding him. She'd cast a spell.

Damn it, she was a *witch*.

Noah's palm pressed automatically to his chest, shielding his wolf medallion. Witches trouble. Big trouble. The sooner Noah got Marlowe out from under her feet, the better.

"This won't happen again, ma'am." He half-growled it, his inner wolf close to the surface.

"And how do I know that, Mr. Blackwood?" She looked down her long nose at him, a difficult feat considering Noah was almost a foot taller.

He was angry Marlowe had put him in this situation. He wanted nothing more than to take the boy and leave, but witches took careful handling. "Let me talk with the boy. You'll see."

She waved a hand. Marlowe staggered as if released. Noah's hackles rose. A witch who could manage to freeze a wolf was no mere dabbler.

Marlowe dared to snarl at him. The idiot.

Noah seized the pup by the scruff of the neck. Marlowe swung at him with the pink rod.

Noah saw red. The pup wasn't an idiot, he was an imbecile. He snatched the rod from Marlowe's hand and hoisted the pup until his legs batted air.

Snarls changed abruptly to thin whines. Noah set the rod gently on the display case. A doodad in a magical store full of doodads that did who-knew-what, and the pup had been swinging it like a bat. Barking dogs, he didn't know how close he'd skated to disaster.

Noah gave the pup a good scold, letting his roiling anger and alarm bleed into his tone. When he set him down, he rapped his nose for good measure.

The boy slouched, as if his tail were tucked between his legs.

Noah turned to the witch. "I'm sorry for the boy's behavior, Ms. Blue. Naturally, I'll pay for any damages."

"Well..." She rocked on her toes and Noah could see her mind working. He waited for the worst, but her plump cheeks went rosy. "If it can make us friends...apology accepted."

"Thank you." Friends? With a witch? He'd rather pal around with a rabid badger. "I'm glad to have this settled."

He grabbed Marlowe by the shoulders and marched the pup toward the door. The witch hustled past them to open it.

She misjudged the distance and plowed into them both. Noah twisted to catch her from falling.

She blinked up into his eyes, beaming. "Oh, thank you!"

That girlish batting disoriented him just long enough for Marlowe to twist and duck away.

The pup, laughing, ran to grab the dildo then dashed toward the back of the store. His running fist pumped the tower in the air like a bizarre personal barbell.

"My vibrating skyscraper mushroom!" the witch cried.

"Mushroom?" Marlowe, as if *trying* to aggravate the damned witch, turned and crowed. "It's a psycho dildo 'shroom!"

The witch flitted after the pup, spinning her fingers like a thousand itsy bitsy spiders, her jewelry clacking like an antique train. "One for the money, two for the show."

Noah launched himself after her. Twist his tail, she was casting a spell. She looked sweet but if she had real power, well, he'd seen the destruction of mages' battles. "Don't—"

"Three to get ready and four—"

"No!" Dread kicked Noah to leap for the boy.

"—to go!"

He cut eyes back. Air warped toward him, wavering like hot day. Before it hit, Noah tackled the boy, taking him to the floor. The impact took the dildo from his hands, flying in an arc through the beaded curtain of the back doorway.

Noah raised his head.

The warped air rippled past them, sailing into a free-standing Snow White oval mirror near the doorway.

The spell rebounded off the mirror. No, the mirror didn't just bounce it. It augmented it.

Noah shoved to his hands and knees as a glittering tsunami of magic whooshed out of the mirror, heading off to his left. Damn it, this was why he hated magic. Unpredictable, uncontrollable. The spell shot into a glass curio cabinet full of pictures, hit one, and ricocheted—

Straight into his face.

It punched him like a fist. He spun on his knees and fell onto his back, magic shivering into his skin like a thousand tiny barbs. The spell spiraled down into him, condensing in the middle of his chest...and then nothing.

While Noah lay there panting, Marlowe leaped to his feet and disappeared through the beads.

Barking dogs. The pup had probably scooped up that damned mushroom on the way.

Noah wrestled to his elbows. His face hurt like he'd taken a fist. The witch packed quite a wallop for looking like a long-nosed Mrs. Santa.

Weaving fingers fluttered in his face.

Acid splashed into his belly. "Lady, don't—"

"Reveal." She stared down at him in plate-eyed horror as her face drained of all color.

"*What* in blazes is going on?" His words were more growl than voice. Normally, he had excellent control of his wolf. But this, on top of being forced into the alpha fight and the challenges to his new leadership, would make even the calmest wolf howl. He shoved himself to his feet. "What did you hit me with?"

The witch's fingers covered her mouth. "You felt that? Oh my. Oh dear. This is not good. This is very not good."

"If you don't tell me what—"

"Nothing. Everything." The plump woman flitted to the mirror. She traced its dark wood frame with fluttering fingers, her eyes surprisingly intent.

"Lady, I don't know what you're talking about. But that was some serious magic."

She whirled, skirts flying. "How do you know that?"

"Same way I know you're a witch." He tapped his nose.

"That's impossible. No one can sense a witch."

He shrugged. "I can. I'm pack alpha." The truth, in so far as it went.

She whirled back to the mirror, studying it so intensely Noah was surprised it didn't blush. She was muttering to herself. "Impossible. Magic is paradox. Witches *sense* the paradox but shifters *are* the paradox. A shifter sensing magic would be like...like a color sensing itself."

Typical witch. No real answer. "Just tell me what you hit me with, Ms. Blue."

The witch's cheeks pinked. "Call me Linda."

He tapped his dwindling reserve of patience. "Nice to meet you, Linda. I'm Noah—stop that!"

She wagged fingers at him, muttering.

Noah stepped sharply back, too late. The spell hit him with a brief glitter. "Damn it, I hate sparkles."

"You *saw* that?" Her eyes widened like hobbit doors. She spun, trotted to the curio cabinet, opened it, picked one of the pictures and carried it back to him. "It hit Sophia's photo before it struck you. Do you know her?"

Sophia. The name rang like the purest bell in his mind.

Then she pushed the picture into his nose, and the woman's face hit him harder than the spell. Sophia.

Smooth, elegant, so beautiful he wanted to howl. Glossy bronze curls, elegant nose, and eyes that hit him in the gut. Big and intelligent, yet hinting that if a man got her someplace private they'd do some amazing things—

Noah backed away. He'd *never* heated up that fast. Damn it, what had the witch done to him? He tried to speak, but nothing came out. He swallowed and tried again. Still nothing.

Desperate to hang onto his control, he closed his eyes and used his three-two-one descent to his quiet place, one of the few things he'd kept of his father's. After dipping a toe in the cool, calm waters of rationality, he opened his eyes again on the witch. "No. Never met her."

She tapped the frame against her lip. "Interesting."

"Linda, enough. *What hit me?*"

"The tiniest of hexes." She bustled to put the picture back then trundled to an armoire to lift a folded white sheet from the shelves. "A simple bur."

He shook his head. "That didn't hit like a bur."

"Yes, well, it took a few detours first." She closed the cupboard, trotted to the mirror and threw the sheet over it. The cloth slithered into place like silk. She twitched a few places to cover the mirror completely. "There, that's taken care of. I—oh dear."

She stared at the front door.

"What's the matter...*yip*?" Suddenly dizzy, he pressed a hand to his head. Or tried to. A paw wavered in front of his face.

"We're closed." Linda's tone was strained.

Noah shook his head to clear it. He felt so strange. He finally managed to focus on the front door where a woman stood, hands over her mouth, staring at *him*.

The woman stuttered, "The door was open and I... D-did that man just turn into an animal—?"

Noah froze. Had he shifted without meaning to? That hadn't happened since he was in diapers. He reached for his human...and nothing happened. What was going on?

"No, no. That's an illusion." Linda bustled to the woman and turned her away. "All mirrors and such. Come back tomorrow." She hustled the woman out, closed the door and collapsed back against the jamb, hand against her forehead.

"Mr. Blackwood. Noah." Heaving a breath, she straightened and trotted toward the back of the store. "You stay here. I have to go check out a few things."

"Yip?" He couldn't quite believe what he was hearing.

"I'll be back as soon as I can." Then, in a flurry of hairpins and a rattle of beaded curtain, she was gone.

"Yip yip...? Yip!" He ground his teeth. Witches. Couldn't trust the lot of them. Always secretive, and not in the necessary, protecting-the-pack way. He started after her, using the long-legged lope that was his wolf's stride...and upended, landing on his back, little furry legs batting above him.

That was when he found out he was a fifteen-inch dog.

Enjoy the following chapter for
Mary Hughes's Pull of the Moon novel

Mind Mates

Now available from 7th Octave Publishing

Pretty little shifter, wizard prince—their taboo love could burn the barriers between worlds.

Mind Mates
© 2016 Mary Hughes

Pull of the Moon Book 4

Shifter Emma Singer has more problems than she can shake her pretty wolf tail at. Her father has been executed, and her mother and brother plan to sell her to a pack alpha for his harem. Even the wicked little crush she has on her boss is doomed—why would six-and-a-half feet of hot, handsome, royal wizard want a boring, good-girl, iota shifter like her? Not to mention her only power is going berserker—that's a real relation-shipwreck!

Gabriel Light is a wizard prince who turned his back on his exceptional powers after he was accused of causing his parents' death. Now he pours his intellect into his tech business, and hides his naughty, forbidden lust for his pretty shifter clerk. But when his sister is imprisoned, and Emma is kidnapped, it's time for this alpha-geek wizard to decloak with all laser cannons blazing. Only one problem—with Emma at his side, how can he stay focused, with his inner wolf howling to have her?

Emma's father left behind a journal. When Gabriel and Emma accidentally release its hidden magic, they learn that together, they hold a key to power beyond imagining—if they can stay alive long enough to use it. But when Emma unleashes her berserker wolf on their enemies, can Gabriel draw her back from the brink before she destroys everyone in her path?

Warning: Contains a hot wizard prince panting to bring out a good-girl shifter's naughty side. Accidental voyeurism, deliberate orgasms, a jealous rival wizard, and fun with prophecy

Enjoy the following chapter from *Mind Mates*:

Swaying atop the three-story ladder, Emma Singer swallowed hard and forced herself to climb higher.

Her fingers curled tighter around the rungs as she neared the metal braces of the Choice Buy's exposed-structure ceiling. An Employee Appreciation Day banner drooped from her clenched hand.

"Damn. This good-girl shtick is getting old."

Wolf shifters, even iotas, weren't afraid of heights, but her stomach slid toward her legs the higher she got, maybe knowing something she didn't.

She glanced down and immediately wished she hadn't.

From the hushed, rarefied heights, her fellow Techie Titans looked like ants gathered around the home-theater setup, where their boss was installing a game. The huge flat-panel was reduced to postage-stamp size by her height.

Strangely, her six-foot-five boss looked just as imposing as usual.

"Hurry up, Emma." Brant the Blundering, the gangly teen who'd pulled down the streamer in the first place, called from the base of the ladder. He was built like a puppy who hadn't grown into his paws—and was as coordinated too.

Swallowing her vertigo, she stretched to refasten the crepe paper to a joist.

"More to the right." Brant waved an arm to demonstrate, hand like an oven mitt on a broomstick.

He hit the ladder and knocked it sideways.

Emma tottered, arms pinwheeling. The streamer fluttered away, waving mockingly in crepe paper's version of the finger.

No good deed goes unpunished flashed through her thoughts as she toppled off. The ladder rocked a few times before righting itself with a *kerchunk*.

It seemed an eternity for Emma to fall the three stories. Below, Brant's wide eyes followed her descent. She had time to wonder if there was a twelve-stepper for acute volunteeritis.

Well. This is gonna hurt.

"Emma!" In the nick of time her boss, Dr. Gabriel Light, swooped in, doing his usual hero thing.

He caught her.

She landed in his strong arms (no problem). They were tight around her (no problem). His scent, masculine and heady, filled her sudden sucked breath (still no problem, or not much of one).

Automatically she clung to his broad shoulders, hard muscles under her fingers, her inner wolf wagging its tail (starting to be a problem). Her fingers threaded into his silky hair (definitely trekking into problem territory). Her lips, a whisper from his chiseled jaw, his delectable earlobe, opened, her tongue aching to swipe a taste.

Red-alert problem.

"Emma, you're safe. Trust me." Behind his plain glasses, his lids lifted to her. His irises were a startling, star-shot blue-green, like the moon sparkling off a warm sea, making her want to dive in and do the breaststroke.

For all that he dressed like a junior college professor, the man was teeth-achingly beautiful.

She tried to swallow, but her tongue had swollen to fill her mouth and nothing happened. She tried again, managing to pant and gulp at the same time, swallowed wrong, and started coughing uncontrollably.

Dr. Light set her on her feet—by sliding her down his sleek, muscular, cotton-and-male-smelling chest, oh *yum*—and rubbed her between her shoulders to ease her.

His big, warm palm did ease her cough, but the breadth of his hand filled the entire area between her shoulder blades and made the rest of her clench with aching desire. Gabriel Light wasn't simply lead Techie Titan—he was their nerd king, and he was built like royalty.

The little iota wolf in Emma yipped happily.

But she, her human self, wasn't so pleased. Despite her interest in him, he'd never shown anything more than kindly concern. The last thing she wanted was to be a poor lovesick fool.

But he smelled so *good*.

"Are you all right?" Dr. Light, one arm clasped around her, slid a long, large finger under her chin. Tilting her head up, he gazed deep into her eyes. His own were sympathetic.

She stopped breathing at the oceans of tenderness in that gaze—fraternal tenderness, but so damned gorgeous.

Plus side, no breath meant her hacking cough stopped, long enough for her to wheeze with what air remained in her lungs, "I'm fine."

One corner of his mouth tipped up in a gentle semi-smile. "You always say that. 'I'm fine.' Whether you are or not. You're not a trainee anymore, Emma. It's okay not to be fine. You won't get fired. It's okay to admit you need help."

An iota wolf, admit to being vulnerable? Hell no, it wasn't okay. Her breath surged back in a rush. She was bottom of the pack, and worse, built like a kitten, tiny and cute to the point that she had to buy her clothes in the kids' section at WallyWorld and one of her nicknames was Piglet. She could never *ever* be caught out as needy and vulnerable, surrounded by apex predators all day.

She wasn't sure whether she meant her shifter pack or the six-foot-five walking sex bomb who was her boss.

Human boss, she reminded herself. Who didn't seem to have a *clue* she was interested in him.

"I'm *fine,*" she repeated through clenched teeth.

"Are you?" His gaze shifted to her mouth, and she stopped breathing again. "That's bad for your teeth, you know. Relax."

He eased the chiding words with a slide of his finger along her jaw, the rough whorls of the pad caressing her flesh. His touch raised tremors in her that shimmered down her throat, waking nipples and belly and wolf.

Oh, to grab him, hook a leg behind his, and take him down to the floor—with her underneath.

She was strong and tricky and might have tried it in private, except he moved like he'd studied martial arts and knew what to do. A warrior's grace hinted at an extremely muscular body lurking beneath his sweater vests and slouchy pants. She'd probably only embarrass herself.

Her wolf didn't seem to care. It was panting and lifting its tail, and her human wasn't far behind.

So naturally, when her eyes were big pools of do-me and she was spurting pheromones like a department store perfumery, her alpha wolf Bruiser prowled into the store.

* * *

Bzz-bzzt. A buzz like an angry hornet stung wizard prince Gabriel Light's ears the moment the predator slunk into the store.

Cap'n Crunch me. Gabriel had magically alarmed the door for just such an event, but why now, when he'd finally gotten a semi-innocent excuse to wrap his arms around this warm bundle of soft, sweet-smelling heaven?

Emma. It felt like he'd been dying to hold her forever. Now, with her in his arms, was the first time in months he could breathe.

But that buzzing alarm told him the approaching beast was male, a wolf shifter, and, from that level of sting, Emma's alpha. The beast was not going to appreciate seeing her in another man's arms.

She started trembling, no doubt in response to the alpha's rampant fight-club stench, a musk even

Gabriel could smell. He tried to ease her tension with a joke.

"Hey, Emma. How many tickles does it take to make an octopus laugh?"

She skewered him with a disbelieving stare, icing his flesh. He'd blundered, she didn't understand he was trying to comfort her, *nobody gets my skewed sense of humor...* Then she gulped and said, "Eight? Like, um, eight legs?"

Immediately his world brightened. "Nope. Ten tickles. Get it? Tentacles?"

She managed a tiny laugh, tinkling bells to his ears, and her body relaxed slightly under his arms. "That was *such* a dad joke."

He loved that she, of all the people he knew, actually laughed at his jokes. He smiled into her eyes like a besotted fool.

Of course, that was when the he-wolf prowled into view.

Gabriel wondered how far he could get with the wolf by protesting his intentions were honorable. Probably not far. The creature was only barely in human form.

The wolfman was medium height but had a face like a dented shovel and a body like a trash compactor, his muscles-on-muscles popping in a stringy T-shirt that barely qualified past no-shirt-no-shoes-no-service.

Worse, with the hair sprouting everywhere, nose elongating like a snout, and lengthening canines, this alpha was dangerously pissed.

Hard to reason with a pissed-off wolf. They tended to bite first then ask questions...never.

Yet instead of releasing Emma, Gabriel's hand dropped from her clenched jaw to open protectively on her back.

"The fuck?" the wolfman snarled.

Something inside Gabriel snarled right back.

He throttled it. Whether his own masculine instincts or maybe he'd developed a wolf to complement Emma's, *down boy*. Diplomacy first. "This isn't what it seems—"

"I know." The he-wolf tapped his snout. "Good thing too, or you'd already have my fist in your face. Let her go. *Now*."

Briefly Gabriel clenched his eyes. The wolf didn't smell it, but Gabriel really reeked of desire. He'd magicked up a way to hide the odor because of the Witches' Council.

Witches tangling bed sheets with wolves was a huge taboo—punishable by anything up to and including the headsman's axe. He'd have risked the ultra-close shave, but the Council Enforcers usually hit the female with the worst of the punishment.

He couldn't stand the idea of one hair on Emma's head being harmed.

Trying to deescalate the situation, Gabriel loosened his arms around her. But he couldn't quite let her go. "Sorry, sir." He forced a smile and managed a creditable professionalese. "Store's closed. Private party."

"In the middle of the fuckin' day?"

"Yes, sir. A special recognition celebration." He had a small one every month, but this month they'd had record sales, so he closed the store early, locked the doors, and put on a real shindig. He wondered momentarily how the he-wolf had gotten in. Maybe with the caterers. "You'll have to leave."

"Not without her."

"Sir, what part of private eludes you?"

The wolf held up one ham hand and slowly curled his fingers. "What part of my fist eludes *you?* If I'm leaving, so is my cousin."

Probably not by DNA. "Cousin" was a common cover story for pack members living together, caring for each other, *getting naked together...* Gabriel's arms tightened around the pretty little shifter. The he-wolf growled in response. Gabriel would have to let go of her.

Soon.

At least the creature didn't know Gabriel was a witch. No one would, unless he was working active magic. If the wolfman *had* known, he would've attacked immediately. The Witches' Council's taboo meant most wolves had no use for witches, and some actively hated them.

Let her go.

Problem was, if he stepped away now the alpha would see Gabriel's intentions were no longer perfectly honorable.

Slouchy pants only covered so many inches of rock-hard hey-how-ya-doin'?

The wolf stalked nearer.

Let her go.

Not yet.

Hell and cornflakes, Gabriel had been constantly aroused, ever since Emma started working at his store two months ago. Her pretty face, pert body, and sparkling personality called to everything in him.

What nailed it was that she actually got his weird sense of humor.

The he-wolf prowled the edge of Gabriel's kill zone. Getting steamed.

Gabriel really needed to let Emma go.

But none of it seemed to matter squat, not Witches' Council headsman nor the hairy promise of death, not when his dreams had become reality at last, and he had her soft, curvy body in his arms.

"Dr. Light, it's okay." Emma's sweet voice snared his attention. "I know this, um, man."

She gazed up into his face so adoringly he fell into her big brown eyes, momentarily blotting the alpha shifter from his awareness.

Which was when the wolfman grabbed Emma's delicate arm in one hairy ham hand and yanked her out of Gabriel's embrace.

Yanked her so hard she stumbled.

Fury seized Gabriel. He grabbed the wolf's slab of a shoulder and shoved him back, popping Emma loose. Stalking after, Gabriel tore off his glasses to glare down at the he-wolf. Bad idea to challenge an alpha, but *this beast dared touch Emma.*

The wolfman's ears lengthened and definite fangs flashed. "What the fuck do you think you're doing?"

Gabriel ripped out, "*Nobody* manhandles a woman, or *any* being, in my...in our store." His jaw clenched against his slip of the tongue. At pains to blend in, he didn't advertise the fact that he owned this Choice Buy. Hell, head Techie Titan was bad enough. He'd taken great care to stay under both mundane and magical radars, to the point of wearing glasses he didn't need. Huffing a calming breath, he put said glasses back in place.

"That is my cousin, and I'm head of the family." The he-wolf's eyes narrowed, spitting fire. "You interferin' in family business?"

While the wolfman spoke, his hairy hand dipped behind his back—where a concealed gun or knife would be.

Damn it. Gabriel played the wimpy nerd to humans and potion geek to witches to avoid exactly this.

Mentally, he called up a shield spell. Violence was about to erupt.

"Enough!" Emma wedged her tiny self between them, shoulders back, chin up, and chest puffed like an irate cat's fur. "Bruiser—I mean Bruce. Leave Dr. Light alone."

Gabriel found himself a little surprised and a lot impressed. She was standing up to a wolf twice her size and her alpha to boot.

This was a totally new side to her. In the couple months she'd worked here, she'd only ever been diffident. Eager to please.

Always saying "I'm fine". He found himself even more intrigued with the pretty little wolf. And more anxious to defend her. He started to cut in.

She slashed him a glance, a clear "back off" in her eyes.

He hesitated. If this was a wolf thing, his interfering could harm her pack standing.

Fine, he'd back off—for now. He stepped to the side, a hand cocked near his waist. Not for a gun, but ready to plunge under the sweater vest for the row of charged magical talismans that studded his belt.

"I don't like your attitude, missy. We're going." Bruiser grabbed Emma and hauled her toward the door.

She dug in her heels. "*No.*"

The wolfman slapped her face, so hard it left a red mark on her creamy cheek.

Gabriel forgot all his talismans, took one step, and planted a fist in the wolfman's snout. *Bam.*

Bruiser rocked back on his heels. His hand sprang open, releasing Emma.

Shocked gasps from the employees gave way to a quiet cheer or two.

Mentally, Gabriel facepalmed. He was a crunchy-even-in-milk *idiot.* Yeah, that punch felt satisfying, but it as good as announced that he'd had a raging hard-on for sweet, soft Emma for two months. A freeze potion or calm amulet would've worked more subtly.

Bruiser straightened, rubbing his snout. "Why you...you *fucker...*"

Gabriel shifted his weight to the balls of his feet. This could get ugly.

"You heard Dr. Light." Another male dressed in Choice Buy blue, equally tall with Gabriel, glided up to stand beside him. "Private party."

Male, not man, his black hair and low, growling bass hinting at his panther heritage. This was Gabriel's familiar, Pan, in his human form. If Gabriel had become a powerful battle mage, it was mainly due to Pan's wisdom and teaching.

Which meant the panther was going to kick his butt later for being so obvious. But in private.

Casually, almost negligently, Pan slid a foot forward into a fighting stance. He pointed toward the exit. "Leave."

One by one, the store employees cinched up behind Pan and Gabriel. Gabriel didn't need to see their expressions to know they were glaring buckets at the wolfman, because the bully paled and fell back a step.

Blustering, "This isn't over," the he-wolf spun and marched out.

Pan rolled his golden eyes.

Gabriel jerked his chin at the wolfman, and Pan, reading him flawlessly, followed.

"Thank you, Dr. Light." Emma appeared in front of Gabriel, her eyes shining up at him. "I could've probably handled him, but your solution was much more elegant."

"It was nothing." His cheeks heated. Elegant? He'd been fury-driven stupid and clumsy.

But at her words, something male inside him puffed its chest and yodeled.

She took a step closer, placing fingertips on his sweater vest. "You're being modest."

The chest-beater started fantasizing, picturing her throwing herself into his arms—and bed—in thanks. His cock rose in anticipation.

Before the fool penis and chest-beater could take over, his phone rang.

Two scoops of damn it.

He'd shunted the store phones to the answering service. Only a few people had his direct line. His thoughts arrowed to his pregnant sister, Sophia. "I need to take this. Excuse me?"

Emma stepped back with a nod and a sigh. His cock sighed and stepped back too.

He tapped the headset he always wore in the store. Most witches had trouble using advanced technology—their connection with the basic quantum uncertainty that was magic interfered with anything electrical—but he'd developed spells to prevent such interference.

After his parents died in a magically triggered plane crash, he'd made it his life's work.

In case it wasn't his sister, he spieled off, "Choice Buy, Techie Titan Gabriel Light speaking. How may I help you?"

"Gabriel, it's Sophia." His sister's voice was low and stressed, almost breathless.

His own breath hitched. "What's wrong? Is it the babies?"

Sophia had married alpha wolf shifter Noah Blackwood in semi-secrecy last month, the forbidden witch/shifter coupling in defiance of the Witches' Council taboo.

At first Gabriel was happy for his sister. Noah was a fine male and loved Sophia to pieces. Then Gabriel's familiar Pan had done a bit of research into the Council laws. Gabriel had already known intermagical cavorting was a felony. Life in prison for a witch caught doing the horizontal tango with a shifter.

But a witch princess having children with an alpha wolf? Death sentence.

Sophia said, "The babies are fine."

He breathed in relief.

"But I'm not. Gabriel, a Council Enforcer is about to jail me, and you're my one phone call. I'm accused of *Coeuntia cum Lupo*."

Mating with a wolf. Gabriel's worst fears had been realized.

www.ingramcontent.com/pod-product-compliance
Lightning Source LLC
Chambersburg PA
CBHW030334310726
48979CB00001B/28

* 9 7 8 1 9 4 0 9 5 8 2 4 8 *